THE BLEEDING GUN

9

2000

0

The Bleeding Gun

ED HUNTER

457669

A Black Horse Western

ROBERT HALE · LONDON

ISBN 0 7090 5411 4

Robert Hale Limited
Clerkenwell House
Clerkenwell Green
London EC1R 0HT

Photoset in North Wales by
Derek Doyle & Associates, Mold, Clwyd.
Printed and bound in Great Britain by
WBC Ltd, Bridgend, Mid-Glamorgan.

ONE

The western sky blazed a mixture of scarlet and yellow as the sun dipped towards the mountainous horizon. The air was still hot and the riders travelled in silence. Their shirts were sweat-soaked, and perspiration carved patterns in the trail dust which coated their faces, before finally dripping from their whiskered chins.

Suddenly Max Boylan reined to a stop and held up his hand, signalling the others to do the same.

'You fellas see what I see?' He stood up in his broad bentwood stirrups, pointing into the distance where a stand of tall timber shimmered in the last of the day's heat haze.

'Smoke,' said a scar-faced man, whose one blind eye was covered by a black leather patch. 'White-man's smoke. I'd say there's either a nester's cabin in them trees, or it's somebody settlin' down to camp for the night.'

'Hey, maybe we can get us some supplies,' the youngest of the trio suggested. 'Somethin' a heap better than beans an' that stinkin' jerky.'

'Maybe don't come into it,' Max pointed out.

'We're all goin' to act right neighbourly. We're gonna drop in on whoever that is over there, and grab us some hospitality.' With that he settled back into his saddle and moved his horse on again.

Beneath the lazy plume of smoke curling from a chimney of hand-made bricks, a sizeable log cabin stood in a clearing. Clean gingham curtains hung at the windows, and a flower garden in front of a veranda, informed anyone that a domesticated woman was installed.

'How long will the grub be, Ma?' Philip Dobson asked his wife as he sat rocking his chair on the veranda, and smoking his pipe. 'I'm s' hungry, my belly thinks my throat's been cut wide open.'

Inside, bending over the hearth, Freda Dobson smiled at her husband's remark as she used a stick to remove the lid of the heavy iron stew pot. After giving the steaming contents a stir, she took a tentative sip from the spoon. She thought for a moment as she savoured the stew before swallowing it.

'Mmm … good,' she murmured. Lifting her voice, she answered her husband. 'Ten more minutes, I reckon, Pa. You'd better get up off your butt an' go tell the young'uns t' get ready.'

Her husband merely sighed at the injustice of being a family man, and got to his feet. That was when he saw the strangers emerge from the trees at the far side of the clearing then ride confidently, at a steady walk, towards the cabin.

There were three of them, all mounted on good quality horses.

Philip twisted round to call in through the open doorway.

'Freda … we got us some company.' He stopped speaking and took the stem of his pipe from between his teeth. As if in a dream he noticed the lead rider raise a carbine to his shoulder and take aim.

'Reach high, mister,' the stranger ordered, 'or you're a dead man.'

The smile faded from Freda's face as she stepped out of the doorway, still holding her cooking-spoon in one hand while she smoothed her apron with the other.

'Same goes for you, woman.' This time it was the one with the eye-patch who spoke and aimed a Colt Peacemaker down at the stupefied wife as she stood by her husband. 'Don't go screamin' yer fool head off neither. I can't abide a noisy woman's scream … it spooks the horses.'

'We ain't got any cash t' talk about,' Pa Dobson explained. 'Practically all we got in the world is what we've made with our own hands. Come an' see for yourselves.' He shook his head. 'I ain't lyin'. I don't have any call to.'

'Mister,' drawled Max Boylan, his eyes unblinking as he stared, 'just shut yer loud friggin' mouth.'

'Don't you speak to my husband like that,' Freda Dobson piped up, brandishing her huge iron spoon in threat. 'We're decent Christian folk.'

Max swung the carbine muzzle a fraction to his left and fired. The woman's mouth fell open. She looked bewildered and let the iron spoon fall with a clatter on to the boards of the veranda.

'Freda!' The shocked cry was not heard by Philip Dobson's wife for she was falling sideways, already dead.

A second shot rang out and the murdered woman's husband had joined her in the eternal embrace of death.

Max grinned round at the others.

'Guess I ain't lost my touch. Come on in, fellas, let's see what's for supper.'

'Gee, Max,' the man wearing the black eye-patch grumbled. 'Why in hell did you have to drill the woman? I mean, you could've waited. We could've had us a whole heap o' fun, humpin' her.' Slipping from his saddle he used the dusty toe of his boot to roll the dead female on to her back. 'She's a real fine lookin' gal.'

'Was,' corrected the third man, a skinny, sallow-faced youth. 'Now she's just the same as a hunk o' butcher meat.' Bending down he grinned broadly as he lifted the long black skirt high and peeked under it. 'Yeah it's a pity. She's got the kinda legs that go right up to her arse.'

'Quit foolin' around and belly-achin' will ya?' growled the one called Max, swinging down and tying his horse to the hitch-rail. 'You tend the horses, Patch, and you ...' – he pointed to the youth – 'ain't ya seen a woman before, boy? Let go that dang-blasted skirt. Get inside and dish out what ever grub there is.'

Meanwhile, a couple of hundred yards down-stream from the cabin, the noise of the waterfall tumbling on to the rocks in the river below drowned out the excited screams and laughter of the Dobson kids. For over an hour they had frollicked on the narrow spit of sand which reached out from the bank.

Every day, except for Sundays, they had worked alongside their ma and pa, all through the high heat of summer. It seemed weeks since they had enjoyed the feel of so much clean, cooling water on their skins. Now they were making the most of the opportunity of this brief holiday.

Fifty yards further along the bank, fourteen-year-old Frank Dobson, the eldest boy, sat fishing. His pole was held tentatively over some expanding rings on the surface of the river, where the grandpappy of all catfish was feeding on bugs.

Tense, and concentrating hard, the youth was unaware of his tongue protruding from his lips as he gently manoeuvred his lure into position. He held his breath, watching as the wily old catfish rose slowly, circled and nudged with caution at the baited hook ... then bit.

Frank flicked his rod and struck hard. The line tightened as the pole bent with the pull of the battling fish, and he felt every movement through his hands. So great was his excitement, he hardly noticed the sound of the two shots from the direction of the clearing. His mind was on greater things. He guessed Pa had fired at another jack-rabbit or maybe a 'possum. It was of no account. Anyhow, there was another fish to fry … so to speak.

'Hey, look what Frank's gone an' caught,' yelled Jimmy, splashing along the water's edge to greet his big brother as he strolled proudly towards them. 'It's a whopper fish, with whiskers a mile long!'

In seconds Frank was the centre of attention, as his excited younger kin milled around him, poking at the catfish with exploring fingers, and asking questions.

'Wait 'til Pa sees it,' Sylvia, the eldest girl remarked. 'He ain't ever caught a fish as big. I bet he'll turn green with envy when he lays eyes on that.'

'Come on let's show 'im, Frank,' Walter butted in. 'I ain't ever, in all my life, seen anyone turn green before.'

With Frank leading the way, they trooped through the trees.

'Now you all be quiet now,' Frank warned. 'D'you hear? I aim t' get real close to Pa, and surprise him. I want t' see grassy-green envy in his eyes, when he looks at this fish.'

Just before they broke through the last of the trees before the clearing, they stopped to peep from behind some bushes, looking for Pa.

'Frank?' Sylvia plucked at her elder brother's shirt sleeve.

'What, Sylvie?'

'Look along at the hitchin'-rail.'

'Saddle horses.' He wrinkled his brow. 'Now who in tarnation can they belong to?'

'Frank?'

'Yeah, Jimmy, what you want?'

'Ma an' Pa's lyin' down on the front porch. See? By the side of the doorway. You think they're sleepin'?'

Frank's flesh crawled when he looked to where his brother was pointing. The kid was right, except his folks didn't look like they'd ever wake.

'I'm not sure, Jimmy, but keep it quiet, eh?' He winked then turned to Sylvia, thumbing over his shoulder, back the way they had come.

'Somethin' wrong?' she whispered.

'Don't know for sure,' he whispered back. 'Take the kids back by the fall, and see you keep 'em there 'til I tell you otherwise.'

'But ...' she began, then changed her mind as the sudden intensity of his stare silenced her.

'No buts about it,' he snapped, confirming his decision. 'Just do it!'

'Ain't fair, we wanna see ya give Pa the fish,' Walter, the younger of the boys, complained.

'Here, take the fish with you,' Frank told him, passing the dead river-monster over to him as Anne, the baby of the family, moved in to tug at his trouser leg.

'Can I help Walter with the fish?'

'Sure, honey, of course ya can. It's a big fish and he'll be glad of your help.'

For close on an hour, Frank Dobson crouched in

the bushes, alert for the appearance of the horses' owners. His folks still lay in the same place. They were dead. He was convinced. As the new head of the family, with all the responsibilities that entailed, he felt obliged to force back the tears of grief which threatened to flow.

As the last rays of the setting sun lit up the front of the cabin, there was the sound of men's laughter and shortly after, the three riders emerged carrying sacks filled with stores and other plunder. The one with the eye-patch also held the Sharps from its rack above the fireplace.

Ignoring the bodies, the murderers strolled to the side and, in unison, urinated over the top rail on to Ma Dobson's flower garden.

Afterwards, the skinny one lifted the storm lantern off its nail by the left-hand side of the door. Turning the wick up full, he lit it and waited a moment for the glass funnel to heat. Then he hurled it, sending it crashing in through one of the windows.

Still joking, they loaded the spoils across their bedrolls, and mounted up.

In his anger Frank wanted to run out, drag the killers from their saddles, and kill every one of them. But common sense warned him that was a hopeless dream. He owned no gun or any other weapon, not even a pocket knife. They would kill him too. And what would happen to the rest of the family then? No, he decided. He had to stay alive for his kin's sake. But those faces, he took good note of. He would remember. Then one day ...

when he had a gun.

With hardly a backward glance at the cabin, the strangers urged their mounts on through the flower beds and moved diagonally across the clearing. All three horsemen passed within a few yards of the hiding youth, each unaware of the seething hate they had engendered, a hate which would eventually haunt them.

'Them was sure fine vittles we enjoyed back there,' Patch remarked as they drew abreast of where Frank hid. 'She was a real fine cook, but I'm still of a mind we should've saved her for some humpin'.'

'We've spent enough g'damn time here,' Max Boylan growled. 'For all we know, that sheriff and his posse could have cut our trail an' be pushin' on, makin' up time.'

'Shucks, Max,' Skinny laughed disdainfully as they moved out of Frank Dobson's earshot. 'That old fool of a lawman, he couldn't find his boots if he was standin' in 'em.'

By the time the outlaws had ridden out of sight among the trees, the gingham curtains were burning like torches at the shattered window. Smoke already billowed out of the open doorway, almost hiding the bodies of the couple. Frank raced across the open ground at the earliest opportunity and dashed into the cabin to attack the flames.

Frantically he tore down the curtains with his bare hands, and ran to hurl them outside, where they burned harmlessly, clear of the cabin.

Home-made carpets, a couple of cane chairs and freshly ironed clothing followed in quick succession. Soon the smoke died down as he sloshed bowls of water on the last few smouldering places. He had been lucky to have caught the blaze in time. At least the family still had beds and a roof over their heads.

Paying little heed to the pain of the burn blisters on his hands and arms, Frank manhandled his mother and father inside the cabin, laying them out next to each other on the big brass bedstead. Only when he had cleaned them up, combed their hair, closed their eyes and crossed their arms, did he go to fetch the others.

After many bitter tears had been spilled, the house was bathed in a stunned silence. Occasionally shuddering sobs and sniffs interrupted the peace. They all gathered around the bed, holding hands, staring at the last remains of Freda and Philip Dobson.

After a while the spell was broken by Walter making an observation.

'Pa, never even … see'd your fish,' the nine year old sobbed up suddenly at his big brother.

'Oh, I reckon him an' Ma know all about it now,' Frank consoled him. 'That right, Sylvie?'

'God's honest truth,' Sylvia agreed. She looked across the bed at Frank, who jerked his head towards the bedroom door then nodded at the little ones. She got his message and spoke with more determination. 'Come on, there's all sorts we have to get ready for Ma an' Pa's send-off tomorrow. All of you, out. Get ready for bed.'

From outside, the milk cow could be heard bellowing her discomfort from her stall in the barn.

'Sylvie … as soon as the young'uns are bedded down, you'd better grab the pail, and milk Jemima,' Frank ordered. 'It's way past time. She must be close to bustin' by now. In the meantime, I'll get a lamp and the spade, and then go dig the grave.'

It was a little after ten o'clock on the following morning. Although the sun had not yet reached its zenith, Frank was already lathered in sweat.

After the simple funeral he had sent the others into the house while, single-handed, he had filled in the double grave. He was busy setting up the wooden cross with the names of his parents burned in to the centre with a red-hot poker.

Suddenly, riders going hell for leather, burst through the trees. With guns drawn, they surrounded the cabin.

'It's all over for you, Max Boylan,' a grey-haired man yelled at the top of his voice. 'You an' your two sidekicks come out with your hands up and you'll be spared … till we legally hang ya.'

Guns were aimed at every window and doorway. The sheriff waited a few seconds longer but there was no answer. As his patience ran out, he shouted again.

'It ain't no use tryin' to skedaddle out of here,' he went on. 'We've got you hemmed in tighter than a frog's arse.'

Frank left the graveside and stalked out from the leafy glade the family had chosen as the resting-place for their folks.

'You and your men are too dang late, Sheriff,' he called out, approaching the posse from behind. 'Maybe if you'd done your job properly, an' got here yesterday, our folks would still be alive.'

The sheriff turned, uncocked his pistol and stared at Frank. After a time he cleared his throat noisily, then spat on the ground.

'Oh, yeah … you're the Dobsons' oldest boy. Hank, ain't it?'

'Frank!'

'Yeah, that's right, I remember now. You were just a weedy little fella, all freckles and teeth.' The sheriff squinted in the sunlight. 'You've growed some in the last couple o' years.' His half-closed eyes settled their gaze on the black armband tied around Frank's shirt sleeve. 'Somebody died, boy?'

'Didn't you hear me the first time? Them fellas you're after … they gunned down my folks. Yesterday! So you can put your guns away, there's only my kid brothers an' sisters inside there, and they ain't likely t'harm ya.'

The five surviving Dobsons stood sad-eyed on the veranda, watching the posse prepare to leave, and follow the already cold trail of the outlaws. The sheriff's horse skittered and pranced, eager to be with the others, as he called out.

'Like ah said before, 'am mighty sorry about what happened to your folks, but that's how life is. One minute you is … the next, you ain't. But one thing 'am certain sure of. I aim t' do somethin' about all you kids when we finish this job and get back to town.'

'If only ...' Frank moaned later that evening after he and Sylvia were on their own again.

'If only, what?' she asked, placing the last of the pots on the table ready for breakfast.

'If only I'd had a gun of my own,' he answered. 'I might've been able t' do somethin'. Maybe our folks would've been alive right now if I had.'

She looked him right in the eyes and after a slight hesitation, came to a decision.

'I've got a gun,' she said, and licked her lips. 'Pa gave it me.'

TWO

Frank Dobson scowled, then relented and grinned at his sister.

'Sylvie, you're bent on joshin' me, ain't ya? It stands to reason Pa wouldn't give you a gun. Heck, I'm a fella, a whole year older than you, and he wouldn't even let me have one yet on no account.'

'I ain't joshin' anybody,' Sylvia stated, her mouth a grim line of determination. 'And I ain't lyin' to anyone neither.'

'You ain't?' He decided to play it smart. 'All right, tell me what sort of gun. And where do you keep it, eh? I've never seen it.'

Without looking down, she patted her skirt against her leg, on the right side, just above the knee.

'Right here,' she explained. 'Out of sight.'

Frank's superior grin returned, along with his male smugness.

'Huh! Must be a mighty big gun.' Thrusting his hands deep into his pocket he stalked away. After a few steps, he whirled round to smart-mouth her, then stopped. To his amazement her skirt was hitched up on one side. She gripped something in her hand and quickly let her hem drop again.

'Here!' Truculently she stomped over to push a small pistol into his hand. 'See ... I wasn't lyin'.'

'It's real,' he gawped. 'I've seen one of these, in the gunsmith's window in town. It's the sort gamblers favour ... said so on the card.' In awe he felt its solid shape and weight as it fitted snugly in his hand. Its vertical twin barrels were as smooth as wet soap, as were the bone-handled grips he fingered.

'Fires two shots,' she explained, as if reciting for a school test. 'One from each barrel. Pa called it a derringer. Said if I ever had t' buy any more bullets, I'd have t' ask the store keeper for, forty-one calibre rim-fire ... said a bullet that size would change a man's mind about things.'

'Is it loaded?' he butted in.

'Of course. Pa warned me, pointin' an unloaded gun gets ya shot, so I keep it ready.' She reached out, took the compact weapon from him and thumbed over the side lever. Hinging the snub-nosed barrels upwards, she let two heavy, brass-cased bullets slide out and fall into her hand. 'There. See? Easy!'

'It's not right,' her big brother grumbled. 'I'm the oldest. Everybody knows that. It should've been me who got fixed up with a gun first.' He slumped down on to a chair. 'And you ain't much of a sister, keepin' it a secret from me.'

'Ma an' Pa warned me not t' mention it to

anyone!' She looked uncomfortable. 'It's my bleedin' gun.'

Frank looked at her, then at the gun in her hand. He twisted his face.

'Bleedin' gun? Now what in the heck's that supposed t' mean? What's a bleedin' gun ... eh?'

Sylvia flushed scarlet and averted her eyes.

'It was all Ma's idea. She explained that, after a growin' gal starts to bleed reg'lar every month, that's the time she needs some permanent protectin' from menfolk. Fellas with all them wild and evil intentions. That's why Pa had t' buy me this....' She shrugged as if it meant nothing. "Coz Ma said so.'

More confused than ever, Frank scratched his head.

'I've been bleedin' heaps of times, all over the place,' he argued. 'But nobody's bought me no gun.'

Sylvia's eyes almost popped. Her mouth dropped open as she peered at him like he was crazy. Then she laughed outright.

'You don't know?' She was sceptical. 'Hasn't anyone told you ... anything?'

Her brother flushed to the roots of his hair, clearly annoyed at being disadvantaged.

'Nothin' about me gettin a handgun for bleedin', they haven't.' He glared at her. 'If you know so dang much ... you tell me.'

'Well,' she began confidentially, 'when a gal's growed enough, she start's a-bleedin' ... down there....'

*   *   *

Close on eight days had passed since the double funeral and the education of Frank Dobson into the reason for his sister's *bleeding gun*. Armed with this knowledge, he was no longer jealous.

Frank's working days were just as long and hard as his father's had been. Already the rest of the family had fallen into the same routine as when their folks had been running things. Sylvia was a good cook. Her mother had seen to that. No one had starved and the home was looking good.

It was mid-morning on this particular day. Frank, stripped to the waist, dug around the roots of yet another tree stump which he intended to drag out and further extend the clearing. Suddenly old Hamilton, the plough horse, standing by with his stump-pulling chains already rigged, snickered. An immediate answering snicker came back from the direction of the cabin.

Frank raised his hand and shaded his eyes. He made out the sheriff accompanying three slick buggies, which were driven to the front steps of the veranda. A whole host of townfolk climbed down and looked around as though they owned the place.

There was going to be trouble. He had no idea what, but was certain it was coming his way.

Even before the strangers began to troop into the cabin, Frank had swung his axe and left it with the blade sticking deep in the tree stump. Then clambering out of the hole, he raced towards them.

'What's goin' on, Sheriff?' Frank panted, taking

the steps three at a time. 'Just what d'ya think you're doin'?'

'My job, son,' the lawman answered without even turning his head. 'Just my job.' He continued to hammer another nail through a printed notice he was fixing to one of the upright posts supporting the veranda roof.

'What's that for?'

The sheriff gave the nail one more bang with the hammer then stepped back.

'You sure are an inquisitive kid, ain't ya boy? It's all official. Why don't you read it and find out first hand?'

'For sale?' Frank gasped. 'You can't do that. We ain't sellin' this place to anyone,' he exclaimed, about to tear the notice down.

'Don't try that, boy. That's a county notice, all legal and sanctioned by a judge. Damage that, and you'll be arrested for criminal damage.' He slapped the holstered gun at his side. 'Shoot ya, if I have to.'

Before Frank could argue further, he heard the children begin to wail inside the cabin. It was pandemonium. Sylvia was yelling in her distress, and strangers' voices shouted back at her. The crying grew louder.

Storming in, Frank forced a passage through the crowd, who with notebooks in their hands, inspected the cabin and its furnishings. He made his way to his sister's side.

'Frank,' she blubbered immediately, 'these folks, they're sayin' they've come here to take the kids away.'

'Oh no, they ain't,' he stated defiantly. 'They ain't doin' no such thing.' Furiously, he began to push at the strangers, driving them towards the door. 'Clear out ... all of ya! There ain't no call for anyone t' barge in here.'

'I warned you, boy.' The sheriff whipped out his Navy Colt and thumbed back the hammer, as he thrust the muzzle to within an inch of Frank's mouth. 'You settle down, or I'll blast ya t' kingdom-come.'

Frank had never come face to face with the barrel of a gun before. His stomach churned. He felt humiliated and scared. Sylvia interceded swiftly, wrapping her arms around him, preventing any foolish action on his part.

A gaunt stranger, dressed sombrely in black, with the stiff white collar of a preacher-man, stepped forward. He nodded to the sheriff and signalled him to holster the gun, then laid a gentle hand on Frank's shoulder.

'You want what's best for your brothers and sisters, don't you, son?' he asked in a kindly manner.

'Sure, of course!'

'Yes, I'm sure you do ... we all do. Well, that's exactly what we're bent on doing. They'll be fed, clothed, housed and sent to school.'

'Sylvie an' me can do all that,' Frank insisted. 'No one's got the right t' take 'em from here.'

The preacher shook his head.

'The committee have more than just the right. We have our Christian duty.' He sighed. 'Now, we all know there ain't nothin' on earth more important than duty.'

'Damn your Christian duty,' Frank protested. 'The kids, they're all stayin' put ... right here where they belong.'

Sadly, the preacher shook his head again.

'It's State law, and that says you're too young to look after them.'

'So you'll have to sell this place, young fella,' another man chirped up. 'You're all orph-ans, there's no other way.'

'But why sell our home?' Sylvia began to blubber again. 'We're goin' to end up with nothin' at all.'

The sheriff stepped forward again. He stood arrogantly with his thumbs hooked into the front of his gunbelt.

'Listen t' me gal. It's gonna cost ten dollars for you and each of them young'uns ... every month, until y'all reach fourteen years of age.'

The preacher cut in, speaking to Frank.

'See what we mean? Can you pay that amount every month to the county?'

'Ten dollars? Sure, I'd do my level best,' Frank answered, grasping at straws. 'I'm a real good worker ... ask anybody.'

'I said ten dollars a month ... for each of 'em. Forty dollars. There ain't no way you could come up with that kind of cash. That's why the county's puttin' this property up for bids.'

'No!' Frank launched himself at the sheriff. 'You ain't gonna take 'em, I won't let you.'

The intensity of the boy's attack had bowled the lawman over. He struggled to his feet, drew his gun and thumbed back the hammer.

'That does it, you're under arrest for attackin' an officer of the law and interferin' with his duties. The judge'll give you six months to a year's jail time for that.'

'You can't do that,' Sylvia screamed. 'He's my brother and he ain't done nothin' except stick up for us.'

With a handful of Frank's hair grasped in his hand, and his Colt pushed painfully under the boy's bare ribs, he propelled him outside, with Sylvia following. The sheriff snarled back at her,

'For a little gal, you surely have a mighty big mouth. Now get to hell back inside and let me do what I have to.'

'Better do what he says, Sylvie,' Frank advised. 'He thinks he's a real big man around here.'

At that, the lawman jerked the youth almost off his feet and shook him by the hair as though he was a piece of rag. Then he pushed him hard against the side of a buggy and slapped the side of his head with his pistol barrel. For a second or two Frank sagged, but held on to the wheel, refusing to give his attacker the satisfaction of seeing him fall in the dust.

'Looks t' me like big mouths run in your family,' the sheriff pointed out. 'Now get up in that buggy and sit quiet if ya don't want your hide ventilatin' with lead.'

By now, everyone had spilled out on to the

veranda to watch what was going on.

'I'm gonna have to commandeer your buggy, to take this prisoner in, Joe,' the sheriff called to one of the businessmen. 'Ride my horse back, will ya?'

The man just shrugged and nodded.

'Can't any of you do anythin'?' Sylvia implored the onlookers. 'You, mister.' She pointed at the preacher. 'You know this is all wrong. My brother don't deserve to go to jail ... not for wantin' to protect and care for his family.'

'I'm a man of God ... your brother's a concern of the law. The sheriff's the law ... you'd better work things out with him.'

Dumbfounded by his cold-hearted reply, she was about to say more but he turned his back and retreated into the cabin. The others followed, as if unwilling to be asked similar questions, leaving the veranda deserted.

The lawman prepared to handcuff Frank Dobson's wrists to the backrest of the driving seat of the buggy, while the tearful girl gazed on in total disbelief.

As though in a nightmare, Frank Dobson felt the iron bands' ratchet closed, and lock, gripping his wrists and biting into his flesh. Twisting his head, he glanced at his sobbing sister, as the sheriff climbed to the driving seat and took the reins.

'I wish I had a bleedin' gun,' Frank shouted. 'I'd use it.'

The lawman laughed, and slapped the reins on the horse's hindquarters to get it moving.

'Yeah, I bet you would, boy ... but you ain't got one an' it'll be one hell of a long while before ya do.'

Sylvia watched the buggy gather speed as it headed for the track through the woods. She hesitated, but not for long. As soon as the sheriff and her brother were out of sight, she lifted her skirts and ran as fast as she was able. Making across the clearing at right-angles to the path the buggy had taken, she ran in among the trees.

Many times she had played the same trick on her parents, her use of the short-cut always beating them in the past. But this time, it wasn't a friendly wave she was after.

Panting, partly from exertion, partly from fear, she arrived at some bushes beside the track. Grimly, she felt under her skirt and produced the derringer. Using the thumbs of both hands, she pulled the hammer back two definite clicks.

Calmer now, and satisfied it was the right thing to do, she replaced the cocked weapon in its holster and stood in the centre of the track to wait.

THREE

Sylvia didn't have long to wait. First she heard the trotting hooves and soon the commandeered rig came into sight around the bend in the track. Standing her ground, she watched with satisfaction the surprise etched in the sheriff's face as he leaned back and hauled on the reins, stopping only feet in front of her.

'What in the name of holy hell an' tarnation d' ya think you're playin' at?' the angry lawman screamed. He jerked his whip, waving her off the track. 'Stand aside and let me by.'

She remained where she was, and smiled sweetly.

'Sheriff, let my brother go,' she wheedled. 'As an extra special favour for me.'

'You gone plumb loco, gal?'

Undaunted, Slyvia still smiled.

'I'll make it worth your while.' She winked cheekily.

'Ya are loco.' This time the sheriff's tone was quiet and thoughtful. 'You ain't got a thing that would interest me ... have ya?'

'I don't rightly know, but you're a man an' I ain't a little girl any more, Sheriff.' She smiled provocatively and took a slow hip-swinging step towards the buggy. 'I've got everythin' any other growed woman's got ... but mine's not been used yet.'

The sheriff wiped roughly at his mouth with his hand. He twisted sideways, and tugging hard, checked his prisoner's manacles. Raw excitement showed in his flushed face as he wrapped the ends of the reins around the brake handle. Then he smiled.

'Well now.' He started to climb down. 'Maybe you an' me can do us some business after all.'

'You leave her alone,' Frank warned. 'Ya hear me? Don't you dare lay yer filthy paws on my sister.'

'Shut yer stupid mouth, boy. Can't ya see the little lady's pinin' for a man?' Looking towards Sylvia, he stooped for a moment and his grin broadened.

She stopped, grabbed the hem of her skirt then slowly and provocatively raised it. Soon she had exposed the front of shapely legs from her ankle boots to halfway up crisply clean white cotton drawers.

'Come on ... lover.' Her voice was low, sultry and filled with devilment. 'I've somethin' here I know you've never had before.'

Rubbing his baccy-stained mouth with his hand again, the sheriff's eyes glittered as he was drawn forward, panting like a love-sick hog.

'Well, little darlin', I wonder what that can be?'

She let the skirt drop back into place and, at the same time, snapped out one word.

'This!'

The smile quickly altered to a face-twisting scowl as the shocked lawman stared into the two up-and-over barrels of the derringer.

'Get the key for the handcuffs, Sylvie,' advised Frank, shouting from the buggy seat.

'She ain't gettin' anythin', boy, exceptin' what she asked for in the first place,' the sheriff growled, stepping forward confidently and extending his hand. 'Give that toy t' me before somebody gets hurt.'

Sylvia, her arms extended in front of her and held ramrod-stiff, pointed the gun directly at the advancing man's chest. When he was barely a yard away she squeezed the trigger. The bang which followed, surprised her almost as much as it did the sheriff.

He staggered back and lurched sideways, half-falling against the startled horse and clawing at the red stain blossoming in the middle of his shirt front.

'You little bitch.' He reached down with his right hand, gripped the butt of his Colt, but failed to draw it from its holster. His mouth fell open and he slid down, bouncing his fat butt on the dusty track. Then like a drunk, he fell back until his sightless eyes stared up at the belly of the agitated horse.

'Holy Moses!' Frank sat motionless, hardly

breathing and looking scared. 'You've gone an' killed him. Ya didn't ought to have done that.'

'Did ya want t' go to jail, eh?' She was unmoved. Gazing in wonder at the tiny gun, she sniffed curiously at the used barrel and smiled, bemused by the newly discovered power held in her hand. Slipping the pistol back into its holster she knelt beside her victim and calmly searched through his pockets.

'There ain't no keys.'

'There's got t' be,' her brother urged. 'Look again, proper this time.'

'There ain't I tell ya, I've looked good. He must've left them back at the jailhouse or some place else.'

They became aware of shouting, the rumble of wheels and the thunder of galloping hooves further back along the track.

'It's the others,' Frank said, checking back down the trail. 'They'll have heard the shot. Come on, let's get goin', before we get ourselves lynched.'

With her brother still manacled to the back of the seat, she scrambled up beside him. Exhilarated by the approach of this fresh danger, she grabbed the reins and cracked the whip.

Startled by the sting of the lash, the horse reared, then lunged into action. The buggy lurched twice as the nearside wheels rolled and bounced over the unprotesting body of the sheriff. The horse galloped, but not fast enough for Sylvia, who alternately clicked her tongue and cracked the whip in rapid succession, driving it on to greater efforts.

Bracing her feet against the footboard, she drove with scant regard for safety. Her eyes glittered star-bright and she dismissed her elder brother's urgent warning with a wild laugh.

'They ain't gonna catch me an' you, Frank. Nobody's gonna send us to no orphanage. No, sir, or put ropes round our necks neither.' With her long hair blowing freely in the wind, she drove helter-skelter leaving a cloud of dust in their wake. 'You an' me, we'll show 'em all what us Dobsons are made of. And soon as we can, we'll have the rest of the kids out with us.'

They knew every creek and canyon backwards, and soon outwitted the townies. Having shaken the outraged citizens of Yellow Rock off their trail, the relieved fugitives reduced the horse's pace to a gentle trot.

'You're brainless. You should've taken his gun for me while ya had the chance,' Frank moaned. 'That was real stupid, leavin' it.'

'Huh, look who's talkin' about stupid.' Sylvia gave him a superior smirk. 'I ain't the one chained like a dog to the back of a buggy seat.'

'We'll have to get these things off,' Frank insisted as soon as they had stopped. 'Ya sure the sheriff didn't have the key?'

'Talkin' about stupid,' she sighed. 'For a big brother you sure say some dumb things.' Sylvia rolled her eyes skywards. 'Course I'm sure ... and even if I wasn't, there ain't no way we're goin' back to find out.'

'Well, somehow we'll have to break the back of this seat. I can't stay like this all day ... besides, I need t' go.'

'Go, Oh, I see.' She giggled. 'Now that could be really awkward for ya.' Inspecting the stout construction of the driving seat, she scratched at her head before placing her hands on her hips. 'How we goin' to do it, eh? You're the fella, you're the one who's supposed t' know these things.'

'If we had us a long fence post,' Frank began.

'Well, we ain't,' she butted in. 'We got plenty of trees around, but no axe. So big brother, you'd better think on another notion.'

Frank's brow wrinkled. He pondered, then smiled.

'Yeah ... trees. That's it. We'll use a tree.' He nodded at an ancient distorted oak which, in its sapling days, had branched into two, close to the ground. 'Drive us over beside that. Get real close.'

Once again she found herself meekly taking orders. The situation had reverted to normal. Frank had resumed his position as head of the family.

'Closer. Get the seat hard up, level with the fork in the trunk. Good. Unhitch the horse, take him round t' the other side, then lead the traces through the gap and fix 'em good to the seat rail.'

Satisfied, he braced himself, then nodded.

'Make him pull ... use the whip. Yeah, that's the way. Keep it heavin' steady.'

The buggy was dragged sideways and tipped up against the tree. As the horse was urged on, the backrest of the driving seat creaked, bent, then splintered, freeing Frank from its confines. The buggy bounced back on to its wheels. He ran gratefully for the bushes.

'Hey, Sylvie … hitch up again,' he called out from cover. 'We're movin' on. Got t' find us a file or somethin'. Until I get rid of these handcuffs, we can't mix in among normal folk.'

Keeping their eyes skinned for any posse, they skirted round the town and headed west. By sundown they had left their past behind and were soon travelling through territory unknown to them.

'I'm bushed.' Sylvia yawned and rubbed hard at her arms after she had pulled up to let the horse drink at a muddy stream.

'Me too. My backside's sore and I'm hungry enough to eat alongside pigs,' Frank admitted. 'And this pesky wind a-blowin' up, it feels cold enough to freeze the drops on yer nose-end.'

'That's for sure. We'll have t' find shelter of some sort soon,' she reasoned, pointing to his shackled hands. 'If it wasn't for them iron bangles you're wearin', we could stop by some place, and ask for hospitality.' She backed the horse away from the water, turned the animal towards the dying sun and headed out again. 'A barn or somethin' like that'll do. Anythin', to keep us warm, and away from nosy folks with small minds and big guns.'

Coyotes had been crooning at the moon for the best part of an hour. Frank, shivering from the cold and with his back aching because the seat no longer had a backrest, broke the silence into which he and his sister had lapsed.

'A light. See, there to the left. About a mile … maybe a mite more or less.'

'Think we should go round and give it a miss?' Her voice was edged with doubt. 'It's a risk. Could waste us a whole heap of time.'

'Time's all we got. What's t' lose?' he pointed out. 'And we ain't goin' nowhere special. Is we?'

'Not if we get ourselves caught we ain't. If you ask me, I think we should either go there on foot, an' take a careful look-see. Or, forget all about it and keep movin' on 'til daybreak.'

'We ain't forgettin'. Frank was adamant. 'We're goin' there. Don't know about you, but I need shut-eye, and so does the horse. Without him we've no chance.'

Having drawn near to the light, they could tell it shone out of the window of a sod-built cabin.

'Can ya see anyone?'

'Not so far,' Sylvia whispered back as, now on foot, and bent double, they crept closer to the frugal single-roomed shack.

'Mmm, that's mighty queer, it's empty,' Frank whispered, pressing his face against the grimy dust-coated window. 'Nope. Whoever owns this pigsty, ain't in there now.'

'But the lamp's lit. Wonder where he is, eh?'

'Right behind you, little lady,' a gruff male voice growled. 'And this thing that's pointin' your way, is what's known around here as a gun.' He giggled like a madman. 'Both of ya, get yer hands up real slow. High. Higher than that. Now you move on ahead o' me, over to the door an' step inside.'

'Whoever ya are, mister, we don't aim on makin' any trouble,' Frank began. He was cut short as the gunman spotted the light glinting on the handcuffs.

'So that's it … you're on the run. Outlaws, eh? It figures, the way you was sneakin' up on me, at this time o' night. What ya half-growed despera-does wanted for? Murder?' Giggling again at his own joke, he pushed them into the shack. Sylvia winced at each bruising prod in her back with the muzzle of his hand gun, but endured the pain in silence.

The door was slammed behind them. They found themselves in an evil-smelling, venomous hovel, no doubt infested with bed-bugs and ravenous fleas.

'Stand over there, against the wall.'

'Ya didn't ought to do this, mister.'

'Shut up!' The man waving the gun sat on the table and rested a foot on a rough wooden stool. Almost bald, what hair he had hung lank and greasy about his shoulders. His skin was coffee-coloured by a long established mixture of ingrained dirt and sweat. Around his mouth and chin, open sores oozed pus where scabs had been scratched off. 'Where ya from?' He looked directly at Sylvia. 'Come far?'

'Yella Rock Falls. Our folks had a holdin' there.'

'Kick ya out?'

'They died … murdered.'

'So that's why ya on the run. Killed yer folks.'

'Mister, we did no such thing,' Frank snapped back. 'We ain't animals.'

'Then why you wearin' iron on your wrists? You like jewellery or somethin'.' The stranger laughed again, his gums displaying more gaps than rotten teeth. 'What ya done that has you hittin' the trail at this time of night?'

'The sheriff planned on takin' us to the county orphanage,' Frank explained. 'We didn't wanna go.'

Already, the stranger seemed to have lost interest in his last question. Instead he eyed Sylvia. After a while, he wagged the barrel of his Adams at her.

'You got the pox?'

'No, I ain't,' she almost screamed back.

'Too bad.' He tut-tutted and grinned. 'I have.' Then he snapped at Frank. 'You. Over here.' He stood and pushed the stool across the floor with his foot to where a side of bacon hung from a hook in a beam. 'Lift that side down.'

Once the bacon was laid on the table, Frank was motioned back to the stool.

'Stand on that, boy. Lift them handcuffs over that hook.' As Frank hesitated, the man came from behind and pushed the pistol muzzle up under the youth's almost hairless chin, forcing him to do as ordered.

'There, that's better, ah just knew ya could do it.' The gap-toothed mouth formed a grin again as with vicious delight, he hooked the toe of his boot behind a leg of the stool and dragged it away.

'Aaah!' Frank's unavoidable exclamation of pain brought tears to his sister's eyes. She stared in horror as he swung with his feet clear of the ground. blood ran down his arms from the skin split and rippled up his wrists by the dead sheriff's handcuffs.

'Let 'im down … I beg ya, mister,' Sylvia pleaded.

'Sure … I'll let the kid down … at a price,' he leered.

'Don't let him near ya, Sylvie. He's got the pox…. You heard him say, didn't ya?'

'Why don't ya shut yer mouth, boy?' The man reached out, and gave Frank a push which sent him swinging, causing his wrists to hurt even more. 'She ain't got no choice. She's gonna drop her drawers. You're real lucky. You're in a prime position. Ya can watch.' He grinned at Sylvia. 'See, she knows all about it. She's hitchin' her skirt up already.'

Indoors, the bark of the derringer sounded louder than when she had shot the sheriff. Fired from only six feet away, her second victim had no chance. The bullet punched yet another hole in his tattered dirty pink long-johns, before drilling between his ribs and into a lung.

The heavy Adams slipped from his relaxing fingers. As it fell, it struck the edge of the stool, bounced off, then rattled on to the floor and came to rest under the table.

The dying man's knees bent inwards, wedging together as he attempted to stay upright. He took a single shuffling step forward. His mouth gaped and overflowed with blood which bubbled with the last of his breath, then dribbled onto his scab-encrusted chin.

'Why?' was all he managed to sigh, before flattening his face on the dirty wooden floor. An outstretched hand clutched at her skirt hem. He coughed, shuddered a couple of times, then lay still. But by then, Sylvia was already replacing the stool beneath her brother's feet.

'Well, that gun of yours, it surely did its intended job that time,' Frank admitted, rubbing his wrists as best he could after he had unhooked himself and stepped down from the stool. 'That's two notches ya can cut in the butt already.'

Sylvia, covering her flush of excitement, knelt to retrieve the dead man's revolver from under the table. The weapon felt far too big and heavy for her hand.

'Here.' She shoved it into Frank's fist. 'Maybe now you'll stop bleatin' about not havin' a gun.'

'Aw gee,' he whispered, feeling the balance of the weapon, aiming it, getting lost in his imaginings. 'Aw gee, Sylvie, thanks.'

'You're welcome.'

Like an indulgent mother, she smiled at his childish antics. Without any qualms whatsoever, she unbuckled the gunbelt and pulled it from under the half-clad corpse. Then she tossed it over to her elder brother.

'Now you're armed the same as me, ya can play your part … an' shoot any dang fool official who dares to stop us from gettin' the kids back.'

'Yeah.' Frank's face was wreathed in smiles. 'Sylvie, there ain't anyone livin' who's gonna push us Dobsons around again.'

New-born bloodlust flashed between each pair of eyes as they met. Sylvia's voice was a mere whisper.

'You're right, Frank. No one.... Ever!'

FOUR

They slept outdoors under the buggy, snuggled down together, wrapped in the same horseblanket from the boot. Rather that, than share their bed with the bugs.

Morning arrived and, stiff with cold, Sylvia went back inside the shack to retrieve the side of bacon from where it had stayed all night on the table. Meanwhile, her brother had other priorities. First he buckled on his newly acquired gunbelt, then feeling at least two feet taller, went in search of a means of removing his handcuffs.

The holding looked even worse in daylight. Everything seemed broken down and uncared for. Even the few chickens that ventured out of the henhouse could hardly bring themselves to scratch in the dust for breakfast.

'Oh boy,' Frank shook his head in disgust. 'Sylvie did that guy a good turn,' he mumbled. 'Killin' him and settin' him free from all this.'

Not until he had spent half an hour wading among the rusting junk, piled up in the lean-to shed behind the shack, did he find it.

'Look what I got ... found me a file,' he exclaimed, bursting in through the doorway of the cabin as his sister, singing happily, sizzled thick slices of bacon in a frying pan on top of the stove.

'And look what I got. Over there, on the table.'

He almost ran to see. His eyes gleaming with wonder he scraped the scattered gold coins into a single pile.

'What in the ...' he began. 'Where's it from? Whose is it?'

'Finders – keepers,' Sylvia reasoned. 'I found it, so by my way of thinkin', that makes it ours.'

He forgot all about the rusty old file and being released from his handcuffs. Frank stood in awe. Then, as though hypnotized, he laboriously counted the money into neat piles of ten coins each.

'...four hundred an' forty ... fifty ... sixty dollars. In gold,' he gasped, stacking the last pile of ten dollar coins at the end of the fifth and shortest row.

'And thirty-seven cents in small change,' she added, slapping down two tin plates of sizzling bacon and flapjacks. 'Come on, breakfast's gettin' cold.'

'I ain't even seen so much money at one time, not in gold or anythin' else.'

'Me neither,' she mumbled, having swallowed a mouthful of half-chewed bacon.

'How come he had s' darned much when this place is so run down?'

'Coz he didn't spend nothin' on it. At a guess, I'd

say he was one o' them miser fellers folks talk about. They sort o' make money their religion.'

Frank grinned.

'If I'd a religion like that, I'd sure as hell pray a lot.'

'Quit yer blasphemin'. Now eat,' she ordered. 'The cash'll still be there when you've got your belly full.'

Stuffing chunks of bacon into his ravenous mouth, he had purposefully avoided letting his eyes stray towards the corpse. But curiosity got the better of him and he twisted around to take a look. In mid-swallow he almost choked.

'Wha …?' he began, allowing grease to dribble down his chin.

Barely concerned, she carried on chewing and swallowed before answering.

'Wha, what?' she countered, with the next forkful already poised in front of her greasy red lips. 'Ya know, Ma said you should never speak with yer mouth full.'

'He's practically naked,' Frank said, after he'd gulped a couple of times. 'Did ya have t' do that?'

'Sure.' Sylvia scanned the room as if to prove a point. 'Ya don't see anybody else around t' do it for me, do ya?'

'But why?'

'Huh! And I always used to think that fellas were supposed to be smart,' Sylvia jeered. Leaning sideways on her stool she picked something from the floor and held it dangling in front of him. 'See? His moneybelt. Had to tear his longjohns and open his pants to get it off, didn't I?'

'Is that a fact?' Frank scoffed, stung by her reference to his brain power. 'Well if that's the case, how'd ya know he was wearin' a moneybelt next to his mangy hide. Eh?'

His sister frowned for a while, then looked down shyly, grinned and told the truth.

'Well, to be honest, I just had t' take me a look-see. I ain't ever seen a proper pecker before. Not a full-sized fella's.' She grimaced and shook her head. 'After all them things Ma told me what it's supposed t' do, I think it's down right disappointin', and that's for sure.'

'We're goin' to have to do somethin', and soon,' Sylvia stated as they sat refilling the empty cartridge cases, after their day's workout on the targets.

Without looking up, Frank carried on crimping a shining lead bullet into its case, then set it in line on the table top with the others already done.

'How d' ya mean, Sylvie?' Reaching for another freshly moulded piece of lead, he carefully cut off the thin flashing with his knife.

'Our money's just about run out.'

'Already?'

'Uh-huh. Already. Money don't last for ever. And I've been as careful as Ma would've been. Ya know that.'

'I can't believe we're close t' broke.'

'Well, I can,' Sylvia snapped, pointing an accusing finger at the newly refilled bullets.

'Powder an' lead don't come cheap out here. Not when ya blaze away every day the Good Lord gives us. That don't bring in any wages.'

'Aw heck, you always come with me. You shoot every day yoursel' woman,' he shouted, in self-defence. 'But the derringer's not good enough for ya now, is it? You have to try yer hand at everythin', don't ya, eh?'

'Huh!' She pouted.

'All right, Sylvie. How much we got left in the kitty?'

'Enough to pay for this room tonight. That'll leave us nine dollars and seventeen cents. When that's gone ... according to this county's law, we're vagrants here.'

'You've got to be pullin' my leg.' He watched her closely and broke into a wide smile. 'Course ya are. We ain't ever gone through over four hundred an' fifty dollars in under a year.'

She didn't smile. Instead her words were terse and little above a whisper as she stared at him, eyeball to eyeball.

'Callin' me a liar, Frank?' She picked up her gun from the table.

He grinned. His handsome face still retained the cheeky look of a boy around the mouth. Spreading his fingers wide, he signalled palm first, indicating she should calm down.

'No, ma'am, I wouldn't dare. Not when you've got your bleedin' gun in your hand. Heck, I'm the only man alive who's seen ya use it.'

Sylvia relaxed, smiled suddenly, and gave her

derringer a final polish with her cloth, before snapping the barrels shut then slipping the gun deftly into its holster.

Frank's self-confidence had increased in line with his skill in shooting. Secretly, he felt proud of his physical strength. He was a man now and knew it. Although he itched to cut his first notch on his gun butt.

Months ago, they had traded in the horse and buggy for decent mounts with more endurance and fire in their bellies. It had been a hard year, always on the move. Never staying for more than a couple of weeks in any one place, they had steered clear of the law. They had lived cheaply, cooking either out on the trail, or eating in down-at-heel boarding-houses.

Frank toyed with the bullets on the table. Sylvie was right. Ammunition had taken most of the cash they'd found. They had practised as intensely as any top-class circus act. Guns had helped them evade the law. But shooting to survive had now grown into an obsession.

Sylvia broke into his musing.

'Another thing,' she began. 'If we don't go an' get the kids out of that orphanage soon, they'll think we've forgotten 'em.'

'Naw,' Frank said adamantly. 'Not when you keep writin' letters and explainin' things to them.'

'Maybe you're right, Frank,' she sighed. 'If they ever received them.'

'Who could stop 'em?'

'Oh grow up, will ya? Any official in a place like

that could stop the letters ever reaching 'em.' She seemed about to weep, but held back. 'Maybe we should've risked puttin' an address for them to reply to.'

'Oh sure, Sylvie, and have ourselves danglin' on ropes just so the kids can practise their letters.'

Frank stood up angrily, banging the table with his fist sending the newly filled cartridges bouncing and rolling in all directions.

'That settles it. Get packed! We leave at sun up. And we ain't comin' back this way without the kids.'

'We'll need money.'

'Then we'll get money.'

'How?'

Frank shrugged, and patted his holster.

'We got guns, ain't we?'

'Yeah ... and we know how t' use 'em.'

Riding alongside Frank, disdaining a side-saddle, Sylvia wore a split riding skirt, and now sat a saddle as well as any man. She was good looking, ripe for marriage and a tribe of kids. But homemakin' wasn't her style.

'We're gonna need cash long before we get anywhere near Yella Rock,' she prodded him as they travelled along a ridge heading east.

'Don't see why. We've plenty of ammo and close on a full gunnysack of beans, jerky and such.'

'We won't starve. I ain't sayin' that, but we'll need money t'rig out the kids when we get 'em.' She glanced sideways at him. 'Where we gettin' it from, eh?'

'Ya expect me t' get a job?' Frank snarled sullenly. 'Punchin' cows or somethin' like that, for a miserable thirty bucks a month?'

'Talk sense. Ya know that ain't no good,' she retorted. 'We gotta go for the big money ... raid a bank or a train.'

He laughed in her face.

'Ha! You got a space as empty as a canyon between your ears. A bank? A train? Let's take on Wells Fargo as well?'

'And why not,' she snarled bitterly. 'The trouble with you, Frank Dobson, is you ain't got no ambition, and no balls neither. All ya good for's playin' with yer guns.' Then she kicked her heels and rode on ahead at an angry gallop.

Catching up with her, he snatched the reins and almost unseated her. He pulled her blowing mount to a savage stop.

'What ya mean ... no balls?' he scowled.

'Well, look at ya. Fancy guns an' leatherwork and ah ain't even seen ya use 'em proper once.' She raised one eyebrow and smirked her superiority. 'Where's a notch on your gunbutt, eh? Come on, big man. Show me.'

Frank opened, then closed his fists. Gritting his teeth, he dismounted, and stomped off heavy-footed to the edge of the ridge. He picked up a small rock and hurled it as far as he could manage.

Sylvia slipped from her saddle and followed to taunt him more.

'Yer all mouth. Always sayin' what ya gonna do, but you never carry anythin' out.' She pushed her face close to his then shouted. 'Well, do ya?'

His anger boiled over and he grabbed her by the shoulders and shook her.

'Don't ah? Well, I'll sure as hell show ya.'

'Oh yeah?' Her pretty face twisted into an ugly teeth-baring snarl. 'Well prove it, or admit yer as yella as an egg yolk.'

'Right. I'll show ya.' He twisted round and stormed back, then leaped into his saddle.

'Frank ... Frank,' she called out, running after him, knowing she had goaded him too far. 'What ya doin'?'

'I'm gonna kill me a man,' he yelled back at her.

'Who?' she panted, swinging easily back up on to her own horse. 'Why?'

'The first fella who happens t' come along, that's who,' Frank snapped over his shoulder, driving his horse into a gallop. 'And as for why, ya know that already.'

Near the end of the ridge about three miles further on, the trail continued down the slope to join a stage road.

By this time Frank had slowed his steed to a steady walk. Sylvia moved up alongside him, but he continued to ignore her.

Worried about the effect her shrewish words had had on him, she resolved to put things right. However, he refused to answer even direct questions, but stared stubbornly ahead.

A dark speck appeared in the distance. It

turned out to be the regular stage. Horses and coach were caked thickly in alkali dust and the driver and guard had their hats pulled well down over their eyes, and kerchiefs tied across the lower parts of their faces.

Frank walked his horse at the side of the dirt road, while Sylvia dropped back, allowing the coach and team enough room to pass on their left.

Sylvia's alert eyes noticed her brother's right hand slip the retaining loop clear of his pistol, leaving the butt sticking out slightly, away from his hip.

'Frank?' she called out. 'Don't be silly ... we ain't planned it. Besides, you know I was only joshin' ya back there.'

'Shut yer mouth,' was his curt retort, as the leaders of the team hauling the swaying Concord were about to draw level with them. 'You're gonna eat yer words.'

Frank held up his hand, and reined his horse to a halt. He smiled up, as the driver yelled 'whoa' and pulled up his team.

The guard lifted the shot-gun from across his knees and lowered the barrels to cover the two riders.

'Yeah ... can I help you folks?' the driver called down from his high seat.

'Yeah, ya surely can, old-timer.' Frank smiled as he pushed his hat to the back of his head and wiped the sweat from his brow. 'First, can ya tell us how far it is to town? And second, we'd sure appreciate a drink if you can spare one. Our canteens ran dry last night.'

'Town's twenty miles back.' The guard peered out through half-closed eyes. 'Ya missed the water-hole over there in Coyote Scar?' the guard asked suspiciously. 'There's always been a good supply there.'

'We found that, but there was a dead horse in it, all swelled up like a pig bladder. We didn't dare risk it. Thought it could've been poisoned.'

'It'll be them pesky renegades who bust out of the reservation last week.' The driver elbowed the guard. 'Told ya, didn't ah? Said there'd be all hell t' pay when the army wasn't called in t' deal with 'em.'

In a blur of motion Frank's double-action Adams left leather and fired without warning. The guard straightened out, dropped his scattergun and tumbled forward, landing between the hindquarters of the last pair in the team and hanging on their harness.

The shocked driver went for his own side arm but a second bullet from the Adams took him square in the forehead and he slumped sideways and hung limply over the nearside of the seat.

'That's me an' you on even scores, Sylvie,' Frank drawled from the side of his mouth.

She watched him. Cooler than she would have believed possible, he walked his horse closer to the coach.

'Everybody out! This side,' he yelled to the passengers cowering inside the Concord. 'Out now, before I start sprayin' a heap o' lead through them windas.'

Terrified, a couple of dude drummers, a middle-aged married couple and two dancehall girls, all hands held high, stepped down and lined up in front of the stage.

'You can take anything you want, mister. You won't get any trouble from my wife an' me. We ain't got anything worth us dying for ... we've got grandchildren.' The grey-haired grandpa reached inside his jacket as though to go for his wallet.

'Hold it, old man. Keep your hands where I can see 'em.' Frank warned. Then he snapped an order at his dumbfounded sister. 'Sylvie, start collectin' what they've got. And stay behind 'em, so I can keep 'em covered.'

Without argument, Sylvia got down and, finding a carpet bag inside the stagecoach, emptied out the knitting and shoved wallets, watches and trinkets into it from the eager victims.

After that, she searched the boot for the cashbox, which she blasted open with a single shot from her derringer. Wasting no time, she tipped the contents into the bag along with the rest of the loot, before holding it for her brother to see.

'That's the lot,' she advised, hurriedly hooking the bulging carpetbag on to her saddle-horn before mounting again. 'Time to go.'

Frank unshipped the Winchester from his saddle holster and replaced his Adams. He levered a round into the chamber, then gazed without emotion at the line-up of passengers. They cringed and all cowered back, the fear of death clearly etched on every face. With grim determination he levelled the carbine at them.

'We gotta go, Frank,' Sylvia persisted. 'We've got what we want.'

'In a minute. There's something I've got t' do.' He grinned again at each of the passengers.

'We ain't g-goin' t-to t-tell on you, fella,' one of the drummers stammered nervously.

'Mister,' the youngest whore whimpered softly. 'Don't!'

'Frank … come on,' Sylvia begged. 'Come on, please, be reasonable.'

'No,' he growled, raising the Winchester to his shoulder, 'I've got me some shootin' t' do.'

FIVE

Swinging sharply left, Frank Dobson fired and worked the cocking lever with machine precision. The women in the line screamed hysterically.

The shooting finished, he shoved the Winchester into its holster again.

'You devil!' sobbed the old lady. 'Why did you have to do that?'

'Shut up! It was either the team, or all of you,' Frank shouted, wheeling his horse to head east again. 'This way you've a twenty mile walk ahead of yers, but at least yer still alive.'

'Yeah, and you two'll have that much start,' the older whore called. 'Kid, I hope we all see ya hang.'

Frank merely laughed, and kicked in his spurs. His horse reared then sprang forward like an uncoiling spring, before speeding along the trail.

Pounding close behind, Sylvia lashed her mount with the reins, the broad brim of her hat flattening back in the wind as she ate his dust.

Shortly after midday they made camp, to rest their horses, reload the guns, and swill coffee.

Sylvia said little, and then only when asked a direct question. But on the other hand, Frank jabbered on about every part of the hold-up from beginning to end. Every word he uttered was in loud praise for himself.

'Now ya gotta agree, Sylvie ... killin' that team was a masterstroke.'

'Yeah,' she sighed. 'I wouldn't 've done it.'

He laughed and slapped his thigh.

'Did ya see their faces, eh? Every one of 'em believed I was goin' to blast 'em t' hell.'

'So did I.'

'Naw, I wouldn't do that. They was just ordinary folks, same as you an' me. Hell, we ain't murderers. Well, not proper ones. We just kill them what threatens t' shoot us, or them that start actin' kinda official-like.'

'Yer a caution, an' no mistake,' she suddenly grinned. 'Next you'll be givin' what we get away to the poor, same as that Robin Hood fella, Pa told us about when we were kids. Remember?'

Frank wrinkled his brow, then his eyes gleamed as his memory dredged up mental pictures of his early stories from childhood.

'Hey, yeah! That guy had a whole heap of trouble with a smart-arse sheriff, didn't he? Some place with a lot of standin' timber an' castles an' all that stuff.'

'Nottingham,' she offered. 'He was an outlaw.'

'That's right. All the poor folk, they done good. Stood by him an' helped 'im steer clear o' the law.'

'You goin' t' gab all day,' she butted in, fed up

with his self praise, 'or are ya goin' to take a look-see what we've got in the bag?'

Before sorting the pile emptied on to the ground, Frank had already settled on a gold watch fixed to one end of a twisted-link heavy gold chain. On the other end of the chain was clipped a gold match holder.

'What ya think?' He stood preening, his jacket held open to show the chain looped across his vest.

'Makes ya look real grand, like a rooster at a county show.'

'Here, you take that.' He passed her a ladies' silver-cased fob watch to pin to her shirt. 'Then we'll both know the time when we're plannin' a job.'

'Fine, thanks,' she replied. 'Now will ya stop yer gabbin' and let me finish countin'.'

'Ya know,' he went on, ignoring her plea for quiet. 'I'm gonna buy me some cigars and start smokin'. It would be a cryin' shame not to put this here fancy matchbox to its proper use.'

'Five thousand dollars. That's sure a right handy haul we made,' Frank Dobson pointed out later that same day, as they rode quietly into the town, seeking a mercantile store for more supplies.

This town was as unexciting as the others they had passed through, with one wide and dusty main street, rutted by wagon wheels and caked with horse manure.

They noticed two saloons, and a livery with its hay barn towering above every other building.

This had a forge attached, but the blacksmith was just sitting out front on his butt waiting for work to come his way.

The mercantile, with a faded red and white striped canvas awning shading its window, had few goods stacked outside on the boardwalk. A white hand-painted message on its window proclaimed a gigantic price reduction ... two cents off a tin of beans ... if the buyer bought two. A single-storey bank on the opposite side of the road, had more bars on its windows and door than the sheriff's office and jailhouse combined.

Linking these main buildings, houses and even smaller run-down business premises, were all in need of a lick of paint. Only the brand new church displayed signs of affluence.

As they trotted past the sheriff's office, a deputy stepped out on to the boardwalk to look them over. Frank, by this time well used to the game, gave him a wave. The deputy waved back and went inside again, his curiosity satisfied.

Outside the saloons, jobless cowpokes leaned on the rails, hardly giving them a glance. They were more interested in smoking, chewing the fat and spitting tobacco juice at flies feeding on the horse dung by the hitching post.

From wide-open bedroom windows, painted bar girls in laced-up corsets and little else, leaned out and loudly offered their wares at competitive prices, to the blushing Frank.

'Must be gettin' close to the end of the month,' Sylvia remarked, as they dismounted and hitched the horses outside the store. 'Seems they're all flat broke round here.'

The brass bell on the spring, danced and jangled above the door of the mercantile long after they had entered. Behind the counter, the owner heaved himself up off an apple barrel. For no obvious reason, he wiped his hands on his white storekeeper's apron. Seeing fresh faces had bucked him up, especially when Sylvia presented him with a neatly written list of goods.

He smoothed his apron. Worry showed distinctly in his features as he cleared his throat.

'You got cash, I take it, missy? We don't ever give credit to strangers.' He smiled apologetically. 'It has t' be cash.'

'Cash! Hecky-me, she's more 'n you got, I'll bet, mister,' Frank chipped in, diving his hand into a side pocket. He rattled a pile of ten-dollar pieces in his open palm. At the same time he deliberately spread his jacket to show off his new watch and chain. 'Give the little lady any damn thing she wants. Right?'

'Yes, sir,' the storekeeper agreed. 'Right away. Anything she wants.'

While the goods were assembled, Frank went out and bought a pack-horse from the livery.

He was leading the broad-backed gelding back to the mercantile to be loaded, as the stage coach rattled in at top speed and stopped in a cloud of dust, outside the sheriff's office.

The passengers piled out and in no time at all there was a commotion fit to wake the dead.

Frank showed no alarm. He simply walked on leading his newly acquired nag.

'The mornin' stage got robbed,' a layabout hurrying to spread the news in the saloons, yelled across to Frank. 'The driver and the guard, both massacred. Gunned down in cold blood. Blowed clean out o' their seat by a murderin' gang o' outlaws, twenty miles out.'

'You don't say?' Frank suppressed an urge to tell the barfly the real facts.

'God's honest truth. If it hadn't been for the incomin' stage, the survivors would still be walkin'.'

By the time brother and sister were ready to head east again, the sheriff had already assembled a posse of armed riders. Amidst a crowd of excited onlookers, he led them out of town like a crazy cavalry charge, heading west in an attempt to pick up the desperadoes' trail.

'Seems to me you were real sensible stockin' up with all that ammunition, mister,' the storekeeper told Frank sagely. 'Folks ridin' the trail need all the protection they can get, these days.' He shook his head sadly. 'I knew them murdered stage men and I ain't likely t' forget 'em. They were into me for nigh on ten dollars.'

'As much as that?' Frank frowned as he nodded. 'Tell ya what.' He took out a handful of coins and selected some. 'Here's what them poor unfortunates owed. And here ... five dollars more for some flowers for their graves. Put a card on 'em sayin' From Frank an' Sylvia.'

'With love,' Sylvia added sweetly.

On the road out of town, a drunken bum stepped out from the shade afforded by the overhang of the saloon veranda. He staggered forward with the exaggerated steps of a full-blown drunk. Hesitantly he doffed his crumpled and begrimed hat and, cringing meekly as he walked alongside them, held out his hat.

'Ain't had me as much as a dry crust all day,' he whined. 'Ma belly's s' empty, it's near reachin' ma backbone for want of a bite t' eat.'

Frank reined in his horse, and looked down benevolently on the bum.

'Say, that's real tough, fella.' He was feeling good after watching the posse raise dust in the opposite direction.

'Frank,' his sister urged. 'We ain't got time t' linger.'

'Sylvie,' he drawled in a voice any preacher would have been proud to own, 'I've always got time to make me new friends.'

'Not tonight, you ain't.'

He ignored her, and made a great display of dropping a fistful of dollars into the amazed drunk's upturned hat.

The drunk clutched his hat hard up to his chest. No one was going to get that hat away from him. Stunned, he backed away, then with a gurgling laugh, sped like a rocket in through the swing doors and disappeared into the saloon.

As they left the town behind, Frank twisted in his saddle and aimed a pious remark at his dumbfounded sister.

'Remember that Robin Hood guy? He always had pals.'

'Great jumpin' Jehosaphat!' The town sheriff tore off his stetson and dashed it angrily to the ground. 'Ya mean while we've all been sweatin' like pigs goin' this-away, the stage robbers've been goin' that? He stabbed his leather-gloved finger to the east. 'Why didn't ya tell me if ya knew?'

The deputy shuffled his feet in the trail dust.

'You're the boss. Thought ya knew. You were there in the office when them passengers were making out their statements and talkin' 'bout it.'

The sheriff clenched his fist and held it close to his underling's chin.

'Don't you shoot yer mouth off and get uppity with me. Hell, ain't you got a lick o' sense, boy? Couldn't ya see I was busy gettin' me a posse together?'

One of the posse picked up the hat and silently passed it to him. Ungraciously, the lawman snatched it and crammed it back on to his shining sweat-soaked head. 'We practically had 'em right in our hands. They must've ridden, cool and brass-faced as ya like, straight by my office.'

The deputy, not as stupid as the sheriff thought, held his tongue. He reckoned if there was to be another murder that day, he didn't want it to be his own.

With the sun sinking quickly behind them, the sheriff led his tired bunch of volunteers back towards town.

'We'll grab us a night's rest then head out again at first light.' He gnawed at his top lip, wincing at the self-inflicted pain. 'This could take days ... maybe weeks to track 'em down.'

'Maybe they'll just travel the stage road?' the deputy ventured.

'And that shows what a hell of a lot of experience you've got, don't it?'

'I only thought ...' the deputy began. But he was instantly cut off.

'Thought? Thought? Boy, you ain't got a thought in your head.' The lawman dribbled saliva down his chin as he snapped out the words. 'No outlaw worth his salt would travel a regular road.' He wiped furiously at his chin with his coat sleeve. 'They'd know it was too damned dangerous so they always cut their own trail.... Savvy?'

Later that night, the sheriff was asking questions.

'I could see right off they were up to no good,' the storekeeper replied, as he prepared to lock up. 'But one thing I'll say for 'em. They paid cash for everythin'. Yes sir, right on the barrel. And in my book, folks who pay that-away can't be all bad.'

The sheriff sneered.

'Hell, Jed. If you made a penny profit off the Devil, you'd write him a reference to be a church minister.' He rounded on his deputy. 'Well, what d' you want now? Can't ya see I'm busy?'

'Sorry, Sheriff. I've got another witness outside.'

'Well, don't stand there. Wheel in whoever

you've got.'

The drunk, by now wearing a ridiculous grin, was supported through the doorway and propped up against the mercantile's counter. Protruding from the side pockets of his ragged coat, the necks of whiskey bottles angled out like pistol butts.

'Hi, Sheriff,' he slurred, dragging out a bottle and waving it unsteadily in the lawman's direction. 'Wanna … wanna drink?'

'Ya know what ya can do with that rot-gut,' the sheriff answered with less grace than a flatulent hog. Then he growled at his underling once more. 'What sort of witness is that?'

'He saw the kids. One of them, the fella, gave him the money t' buy all that booze.'

'Kids? Fella?' The sheriff's forehead wrinkled like a closed concertina. 'You sayin' what ah think yer sayin'?'

'What's that, boss?'

'You standin' there tellin' me we're chasin' a couple of kids? And that the other outlaw ain't a fella at all … that he's a woman?'

'Sure. Everybody in town knows that.'

'Oh sure….' His voice had lowered and the words were spoken in a soft, pleasant tone that seemed to him more than reasonable under the circumstances. 'Everybody but me.'

Open-mouthed and unblinking, the deputy backed towards the door, his hand held behind him as he groped desperately for the door handle.

Slowly following him, the sheriff moved like a zombie. His face had turned purple. A thick snaking vein was pumping visibly on the side of his head. His eyes protruded and he glared with malevolence at the deputy. Then he yelled.

'And I'm the one with the dang-blasted star!'

Having topped the ridge and looked down, they recognized the sod-cabin. But it looked different. The yard had been cleaned up and useful brood mares chomped hay in a newly built pole corral.

'Somebody's moved in,' Sylvia murmured.

'Yeah, but who?' Frank snorted. 'That's what's got me thinkin' on things.'

'What we doin'?'

'We'll sit here a spell and keep an eye on the place.' He broke into a crafty smile. 'Who knows, this place gave us good pickin's the first time. Maybe it'll do the same again.'

'There's a handy-lookin' buggy over by that new barn.' Sylvia directed his gaze away to the north side of the main building. 'Could turn out to be real handy for when we collect the kids.'

A thickset farmer in faded blue dungarees emerged from the barn with a bucket of mash, which he fed to the hens. He spent all afternoon doing this chore and that, never stopping long enough to stretch or mop his brow.

'Sure likes work, don't he Sylvie?'

'More than you do.'

'I can work alongside the best of 'em,' Frank retorted, peeved by her inference. 'But there ain't no point now, is there?'

In a flash he drew his pistol, expertly twirled it

round his finger and had replaced it in the holster almost before she could blink an eye.

'I've got another way of earnin' a livin', ain't I?'

'You better be careful, big brother. You get too cocky with that gun, and somebody'll be puttin' a hole in yer hide.'

'Well, that fella down there won't, that's for sure.' He rose to his feet. 'Come on, let's go down and ask for some hospitality.'

He kept on worrying away at his chores, finishing one, then moving straight on to the next. Not until they were in speaking distance did the fella finally stand up and face them directly.

Frank tipped his hat.

'Howdy. Frank Dobson's the name.' He waved a hand. 'My sister, Sylvie.'

There was no answering smile. Only a curt nod of the head.

'Ma'am,' he grunted. 'Somethin' I can do for you folks?'

'Well, now that you mention it, there is.' Frank slid from the saddle and nodded towards the wooden trough. 'We'd be real obliged if you'd let us water our horses.'

The farmer jerked his head to confirm his agreement.

'That all?'

'Well, not exactly,' Sylvia chirped up as she dismounted. 'I saw that buggy over there. It's just what my brother and I are lookin' for.'

'Well, if you've the money, miss, it's for sale. Yes, ma'am. I've always been ready t'do a spot of tradin' ... at any time.' He walked off in the direction of the buggy. 'Come and see. Make me a sportin' offer.'

While they checked the vehicle over, he disappeared into the barn to fetch the harness leathers.

'It's the one we want,' Sylvia whispered.

'Uh-huh, and it's the one we're gonna get.'

The side door of the barn swung open again and as they turned, the farmer stepped out. Instead of an armful of harness, he held a shot-gun, aimed from the hip, directly at Frank.

'Only use your left hand, boy.... Now careful like, drop my brother's gunbelt, son, before I drop you.'

SIX

Like a doomed jack-rabbit hypnotized by a rattler, Frank stared into the unwavering gun barrels. He attempted to swallow, but couldn't. With trembling fingers, he unbuckled the gun rig and let it slip over his hips to thud on the ground at his feet.

'Now you be careful with that scattergun, mister,' Frank advised, finding his voice again. 'Yer makin' a bad mistake. If ya check up you'll find I bought me that gun and belt only yesterday. Go fetch yer brother,' he suggested craftily. 'Let him check it over.'

'Sir, there's a perfectly good explanation to all this. It ain't what it looks like,' Sylvia burst out, putting on the style. 'My brother'd not harm a fly. No sir, not on any account. And we're church folk. Real Christians.'

The stranger laughed. He coughed, then hawked noisily and spat at a chicken which had strayed near.

'Then you'd better start prayin'.' He spat again. 'You both know my brother's dead. Murdered by you.'

'No, mister. That ain't so.'

'Keep your mouth shut and stay out of this, girl. Hands on your heads. Now move back. And you, boy, step clear, well away from that gunbelt.'

He jerked the shot-gun as a threat. Then, when satisfied they were at a safe distance, never taking his eyes off them, he crouched carefully, and retrieved the gunbelt.

With his left hand, he slung the bullet-filled belt and holster over his shoulder, and waved the twelve-gauge again.

'Get goin', over to the cabin. Go on. Shift yer backsides.'

The rejuvenated sod cabin had altered a lot since Frank and his sister had been there. Now it was clean. There were even curtains at the window, and pots and pans were stowed in neat racks by the stove. The floor had been scraped and scrubbed, then made homely by a scattering of skin rugs.

Frank sighed as the homesteader came behind him and, with one powerful hand, slipped a noose over his wrists and pulled it tight. His arms were straightened above his head, as once again he found himself hauled on tiptoe, suspended painfully from the bacon hook.

'Now you, girl.'

'You're not hangin' me up like that,' Sylvia objected.

'I will, if you don't keep quiet.'

Soon she was sitting on the side of the bed, her wrists bound with thin, tough cord, and secured to the bed frame.

'I've got to hand it to you young'uns. Neither of you are hazed one bit, and as things stand, that sure ain't easy. Yes, ya sure have more than your share of spunk.'

He splashed stewed black coffee from the pot on the hearth into a tin mug, and sat drinking it while examining the Adams at leisure. After little more than a cursory glance, he nodded and tut-tutted.

'Yep, you murderin' bastards. It's my brother's gun all right.' He tapped his fingernail on the frame between the trigger guard and the cylinder. 'J. R. C. They're his initials.'

He strolled over to Frank, pointing to the engraving.

'It cost extra for that. I bought him this Adams. It's a double action. He couldn't use a Colt or any other single action. He'd a stiff thumb.' He shook his head. 'Never would've sold this, not for anythin'.' He paused, his mind elsewhere. 'Aye, poor Jamie. Rottin' t' death with the pox. Might've lived like a pig ... but he kept this pistol clean as new bought.'

The homesteader ambled back to his seat.

'Well,' Frank argued again, 'we don't know nothin about that. I paid good money for that gun in a mercantile ... in that last town, back along the road a pace.'

'Ya don't give up, do ya?' Angrily he got up from the table and stormed back to face Frank. 'Listen, an' listen good.' He glowered, his face inches from his prisoner. 'Jed Harper, he's the guy who owns that store. Been after buyin' that gun for years. Used to badger brother Jed whenever he laid eyes on him.'

He delivered a breath-taking jab with his balled fist to Frank's stomach. Frank gasped and almost spewed up, as he fought to breathe.

'If he'd got his hands on this gun, Jed would've kept it … 'til his dying day. No, I reckon you shot my brother, robbed him and left him on the cabin floor to rot.' He delivered another blow, similar to the first, then stormed out of the cabin.

'You all right, Frank?' Sylvia called in a loud whisper.

'Uh-huh … will be … if I ever get my breath back again.'

'That fella don't like you.'

'You think I haven't noticed?'

'D'ya think he's gonna kill us, or hand us over to the law?'

'What's it matter … either way, we're dead.'

'Well, what we gonna do?'

Frank stared as though she'd been smokin' loco weed.

'Do? Look at me, what in hell can I do? You're the one with the best chance, ain't ya?' He checked towards the door. 'You've still got yer bleedin' gun, ain't ya?'

Their captor re-entered the cabin.

'I've made up my mind. When I first saw you with Jed's gun, I had a notion to blast the two of you and feed ya in bits to the hogs. But then I got t' thinkin', if I did that I'd be makin' mysel' as bad as you.'

'You're goin' t' let us go?' Sylvia beamed hopefully at him.

The homesteader scowled.

'No. I ain't. I'm gonna get the buggy ready, take both of yer into town, and hand ya over to the sheriff. But don't you worry none. You'll get a proper trial ... then you'll get yer necks stretched.'

'They won't hang us ... they can't, we're too young,' Sylvia argued, as usual.

'Oh, you'll hang. In this county there ain't no age limits ... either up or down.' He made for the door again. 'So you'd better get used to the idea.'

Within ten minutes the buggy was ready and brought around to the doorway.

'One move from you ... and you won't have any back to yer head.'

Frank was marched out at gunpoint. Then he was trussed, and fastened down behind the seat so tightly he couldn't move more than his eyeballs.

'Hey, mister. I'll have t' use the privy,' Sylvia informed him as he freed her from the bed. 'I was ready t' go when we got here.'

'No, you hold on.'

'I can't,' she persisted. 'I'll bust!'

'Then damn-well bust.' Gripping her arm, he swung her from the bed and propelled her roughly to the open doorway. 'You wanna wet yoursel', go ahead, that's your choice.'

'Right,' she snapped. 'But remember ... it's your buggy!'

The homesteader considered the pristine

leather upholstery. The rig's value would plummet like a bucket down a well.

'OK,' he agreed grudgingly. 'You can use the privy but no tricks. You leave that door open so's I know what's goin' on.'

'Like hell, I will. You one o' them perverts, mister?'

'It ain't nothin' new. I've seen it all before.'

'Not mine you ain't, and you're not goin' to, neither.'

'All right,' he yelled in exasperation. 'But get on with it. I'll stay outside the door.'

Sylvia took her time, did what she had to and, after a suitable interval, opened the privy door.

'And about time,' he began.

Instant fear flashed in his eyes. He started to swing the twelve-gauge.

Arms extended towards him, she held the derringer firmly in both hands, already aimed. She grinned, and squeezed the trigger.

He was a powerful man and, to her surprise, the bullet seemed to make little impression as it ploughed into his barrel of a chest. He stepped closer, still attempting to bring the shot-gun up on aim. His thumb was dragging the hammer back.

Frightened by his sheer tenacity and the look of hatred on his face, she froze. Only her finger moved and she fired her remaining shot.

His right eye disappeared and blood splashed out from the vacant socket. As the bullet zipped through the back of his skull, a tuft of his hair lifted into the air then floated slowly to the ground. His shot-gun tilted up over her head, going off with a roar which threatened to deafen her for life.

The dead man fell spreadeagled on his broad back.

Sylvia drove the buggy into the town of Yellow Rock. With her hair piled high, and wearing a town dress, she was confident she would not be recognized.

Tied to the rear of the buggy, the pack horse and her own mount trotted in unison. It was early, not long after breakfast, on the morning after her third victim had gone to meet his Maker.

She swung off the road and in to the yard at the rear of the livery stables. Here the vehicle and the animals were booked in for feed, a shoe check and grooming.

Checking her fobwatch, she made sure time was well in hand before seeking a store and buying herself a fashionable parasol and a hat with a heavy-spotted veil.

'Hey, ya look just like a real lady,' Frank told her an hour later, on the corner by the funeral parlour.

He had ridden into town from the opposite direction, just in case he should be seen and recognized. Although he wore a broad-brimmed hat, he had bought a newspaper so he could use it to shield his face from prying eyes if need be. But nobody appeared to notice them anyway.

Like a young courting couple they walked arm

in arm around the town, seeking the orphanage, but with no luck.

'That sheriff I blasted ... he did say it was in Yella Rock, didn't he?'

'I'm dang certain he did. So did the preacherman,' Frank started to shout at her, then sheepishly lowered his voice, remembering how exposed and vulnerable they were. 'It stands t' reason they'd build the orphanage here.'

'Well, we've been through every street in the place twice over. It has to be some place else, don't it?'

It was a few minutes past noon and the sun blazed directly down casting the smallest of shadows. The temperature in the confines of the streets had grown close to unbearable. They decided to find an eating-house, get under some shade, and talk over the problem of their misplaced kin.

Ordering pork and beans, they sat at a rickety table by the window and waited. Frank balanced the chair on its back legs and spread out his news sheet.

'Holy Moses!' she heard him gasp, bringing the chair down on the other legs with a thump. 'It can't be.'

'What's the trouble, Frank?' she blurted out, seeing tears flooding down his cheeks. 'What's happened?'

He couldn't speak. Instead he tried to blink back his tears, failed, and shoved the newspaper across the table. His finger stabbed at an article at the bottom of the page. Then he twisted round, and pretended to be interested in the street outside.

'Last night, the elders of the church,' Sylvia began to read aloud, 'finally agreed to rebuild the county orphanage. Readers will recall with horror how, one night six months ago, the building caught fire. Within twenty minutes of the conflagration starting, every inmate had died.'

A surly, podgy girl with a severe squint, brought the pork and beans.

'Anythin' else?' she asked flatly, thumping the two plates down, without finesse, on the ketchup-stained table-cloth. 'Coffee, tea or beer?' From a pocket in her grubby apron she took the eating irons, breathed on them and made a show of polishing them on an equally dirty cloth. 'Whatever ya get, it costs extra.'

Ignoring the grub, Sylvia steeled her nerves and pointed to the article.

'Is this right ... did all the children really die?'

The girl leaned nearer, closed the eye which squinted, and read.

'Oh, yeah, they're dead all right. They better be, 'coz they buried 'em.' She grinned. 'Got the afternoon off t' go to the funeral. The whole town did.'

'How'd it happen?' Frank cut in huskily, still looking out of the window.

'Well, after prayers, the young'uns had all been locked in the upstairs dormitories for the night. They always did that, to stop the kids runnin' away.'

'And then?' Frank pressed. 'How did the fire start?'

The girl checked around to see if anyone was listening, then moved in closer.

'I've heard tell,' she whispered, 'it was the preacher's fault. Got drunk an' fell asleep by the oil lamp in the parlour down below. Knocked the lamp over and, instead of tryin' to put out the flames, he skedaddled outside like a scared rabbit.'

'How'd ya know?'

'Folks saw him there. It was all over town next day. He was gibberin' drunk, outside in his nightshirt, watchin' the place go up like a torch, while the kids screamed fit t'make a stone weep.'

'What happened t' the preacher-man?'

'What you'd expect. Nothin'!'

'What do ya mean, nothin'?' Sylvia asked, in disbelief.

'He's been livin' high as a prize hog, in a boardin'-house, waitin' while they make up their minds to build another place for orphans, or not.'

The posse stood around in front of the privy to look at the body of the dead homesteader. The sheriff was not in a good mood, so everyone stayed thoughtful and said nothing to inflame his temper more.

'Great Jumpin' Jehosaphat!' the lawman snarled through clenched teeth. Again he dashed his hat to the ground. Once more a member of his posse handed it meekly back. 'These days, it seems all I ever do is trip over bodies left behind by them dang-blasted gun-totin' kids.'

'There's a hole been blowed through the top of the privy, Sheriff,' the daredevil deputy called from inside the cramped confines of that building. 'At a guess, done by a shot-gun.'

The privy door was jerked open and slammed back against the wall, disturbing the dust from the cracks in the roof and falling on the sheriff's upturned sweating face as he stepped inside to see.

'Of course it was a damned shot-gun. You don't think a fart did that, do ya?' His mouth twisted into yet another sneer. 'Or maybe ya think them holes were designed an' made by an educated woodworm?'

Undaunted, the long-suffering deputy waited for the laughter from outside to die down before he continued with his theory.

'Ya know what I think?'

The sheriff rolled his eyes upwards, inhaled deeply then, as softly as a burning fuse on a powder keg, he asked the question.

'Yes?'

'Well, that fella down there, was shot by somebody standin' about here.'

'Yes.' The word was still soft-like, but with a definite hiss to it.

Setting his jaw, the deputy advanced his theory some more.

'If that guy on the ground fired that there

shot-gun and did that to the roof, he wasn't just sayin' hello to the other fella.'

'So?' Rubbing at his bristled chin, the sheriff felt uneasy. His underling was getting to be mighty over-confident.

'So.' His deputy smiled widely, surveying the open-mouthed onlookers waiting on his every word. 'If one guy with a gun happens to fire at another guy with a gun ... and the other guy fires his gun and shoots the guy who fired the first gun ... well!'

With nerves twanging like a plucked G-string on a Mexican guitar, the sheriff waited. The men in the posse waited, and waited.

'Well, what in tarnation are ya holdin' out for? Tell us what yer thinkin' f' Christ's sake.'

Milking his moment of glory for all it was worth, the deputy stepped out of the privy, his thumbs tucked in the armholes of his vest and his chest stuck out. He paraded like a slick city attorney in court.

'Well, if one guy shoots at another, shootin' at ...'

'What's ya friggin' point?' the sheriff bawled close to the deputy's left ear.

'It ain't necessarily murder.'

'It ain't?'

Murmurs of amazement flowed through the onlookers like a laxative through a skeleton.

'What is it then?' Even the sheriff was overawed.

'Self-defence,' grinned the deputy. And with a

theatrical wave of his arm to the rest of the posse, he added. 'I rest my case.'

At that precise moment, Frank and Sylvia Dobson checked their watches and began to stroll past the boarding-house where the preacher had his rooms.

This was, they had been told, about the time he left the comfort of the house for his nightly constitutional walk to the saloon. There, in a small room behind the bar, the pious man of the cloth would attempt to save the souls of the bar girls, or any sinner prepared to split a bottle or a pack of cards with him.

They had timed it well. A tall, gaunt figure dressed head to toe in black, came out of the boarding-house. As he shut the white-painted garden gate they caught a flash of white from his dog collar. Then, with his hands clasped firmly behind his back, he sauntered along the sidewalk, head in the air, and apparently without a care in the world.

The couple walking behind increased their pace and, just as he was about to turn down an alleyway, caught up with him.

'Hello Preacher-man, remember us?' Frank asked, drawing level with the taller man's elbow.

The man of the cloth hardly glanced at them.

'No. Can't say I do.' Before he could turn the corner, Frank gripped one elbow, and his sister the other.

'What in the name of ...' he began. 'How dare

you? Unhand me ... at once.' Something hard jabbed painfully round about where his kidneys had started to work overtime.

'Keep quiet,' Frank muttered, 'or you'll wake every kid in the neighbourhood ... when I blast your lyin' head off.'

The preacher grunted and almost doubled up with pain as Sylvia moved in real close and shoved the snub nose of the derringer in hard, and low down. She raised her veil from her face and smiled up at him like an angel.

'And ya can tell where I'll shoot ya, can't ya ... Preacher?'

With his skin fading quickly to almost the same colour as his collar, the worried preacher took a real good look at his companions.

'Yes, I do know you. You're those ...'

'Dobsons from Yella Falls.'

'You're wanted by the law. There's a reward out for you. For murder and horse stealing.'

Brother and sister exchanged looks.

'Wow!' they laughed. 'Is that all?'

Together they directed him to where the buggy waited.

'You were treadin' the wrong path, Preacher-man. We're gonna put ya straight, ain't we, Sylvie?'

'That we is. Yes sir, that we is.'

SEVEN

With the preacher wedged between them on the buggy seat, they drove at a moderate speed to the graveyard. There, with the derringer pressed against his ribs, their reluctant passenger directed them to the mass grave of the orphans defrauded of their lives by the fire.

The grave was a simple affair. A nondescript plot of land, tucked away in a corner unshaded by trees, and separated from the more affluent areas by a cheap little fence. A single wooden cross, already warped and cracked by the sun, leaned sideways a little at the head of the plot. A few bunches of flowers, long-since dead, stuck into old pickle jars, displayed the only signs that this was indeed a final resting place.

'The church committee sure don't waste cash on the niceties.' Sylvia wrinkled her nose in disgust.

'When folk donate t' charity,' the churchman pointed out, 'they don't expect their money t' be thrown down a bottomless hole.'

'Yeah,' she snapped back like an angry sidewinder. 'Specially if there's only orphan kids buried in it.'

'Not exactly brimmin' with all that good old Christian charity ya once preached t' me about,' Frank reminded him coldly. 'Now, how about you doin' somethin' worthwhile? Show us sinners how you pray.'

The preacher covered his face with his hands and emphatically shook his head.

'I can't. Not here, it wouldn't be right.'

'Wouldn't it now? That's too bad.'

Frank, his patience already at a low ebb, boiled over and pushed the preacher violently, almost putting him down.

'What in the name of hell, d' you know about right?' he demanded.

'Please!' the churchman cowered. 'We're all civilized people here ... not savages.' For such a tall man, he certainly began to look small. By this time he was sobbing shamelessly and shaking his head continuously from side to side.

Unmoved, Frank persisted.

'On ya knees, fella ... no, not down there. On the grave. I want to see ya sayin' prayers where the kids are restin'.'

Scrambling over the knee-high wooden fence surrounding the grave, the preacher snagged his black trousers. They heard the cloth rip, but in his panic to satiate the demands of his aggressor, he paid no heed to the triangle of serge left behind.

Quickly, as though it was what he wanted most, he knelt in the dirt. Placing his hands together, he squeezed them so hard his knuckles showed as white as cold candle wax. Twisting to look over his shoulder, he peered miserably through blurring tears, searching for a sign of compassion in Frank's expression. Loudly he sniffed several times. His shoulders heaved and his whole body trembled with apprehension.

Gone was the gusto of his fire and brimstone speeches issued from the pulpit. Then he had been able to turn mean sinners into generous souls who had kept him in comparative luxury for the past twenty-five years. Now, utterly dejected and without a smattering of pride remaining, he pleaded, promising impossible things ... anything to make amends for the past.

His tormentors stood stone-featured and silent, ignoring his pleas. The hatred in their eyes filled him with dread.

Eventually his voice, hoarse by now, trailed away to a whimper when he realized the words were making no impression on Frank.

In black despair he appealed to the womanly instincts of Sylvia, but she neither smiled nor frowned, but continued to stare, her face a steely mask of contempt and silent loathing.

'Pray!' Frank spoke the single word quietly. At the same time he unshipped the Adams from its holster.

Immediately a wave of hysteria swept over the preacher. Weeping and wailing like a demented woman, white flecks of spittle foamed on his lips, and his eyes rolled, no longer under control.

'You're goin' to shoot me.... You're goin' t' kill me

... I'm goin' t' die. Oh God, I'm goin' t' die.'

'That's right, Preacher-man.'

Frank remained where he was. Absentmindedly he fingered the Adams and spun the cylinder a couple of times. He raised his arm slowly and spoke the last words the churchman would ever hear.

'Now, as you Bible thumpers keep on sayin', the Lord's will be done.'

Two pistols shots occurred almost simultaneously as avenging brother and sister fired.

The executed man threw up his arms and half-twisted as the lead bullets slammed him brutally down, gouging the last years of life out of him. Reflexes worked his long arms and gangling legs, straightening and causing them to shake. His blood dribbled into the dust, as a penance to those already beneath the sod.

Frank fired again and the body jerked some more.

'That one's for little Anne.' He squeezed off another round. 'That was for Walter, and this ...' – the Adams kicked in his fist once more – 'is for our brother, Jimmy.'

As the echoes of the gunshots died out over the graveyard, Sylvia tugged at his arm.

'There's people comin' to see what the shootin's about.' She pulled harder. 'Come on, Frank, be smart, we gotta scoot.'

Refusing to run, and calmly reloading the revolver as they returned to the buggy, Frank ignored the townsfolk who had come to nose around. No one challenged them or even shouted a question. Only when they began to drive away from the gates did somebody find the body and yell.

'Murder!'

'Wrong,' muttered Frank, flicking the whip, urging the horse into a rhythmic canter. 'In my book, that was nothin' less than justice.'

With their future plans now shot to pieces, the survivors of the Dobson family decided to take life easy for a spell. They needed time to think on things. For that reason they returned to the cave at Yellow Rock Falls.

'Maybe it's time t' shake the dust o' this stinkin' county off our heels for good. Try out a new State, somewhere the law don't want us?' Frank shouted as he lounged on a rock, his hat tilted over his eyes, while he wielded a fishing pole he'd cut from trees along the bank. 'We got us all we need t' do that.'

They were not far from where the waterfall plunged into a deep hole, near where the catfish liked to cool off in the shade of the cliff.

'Ya can't mean that, Frank?' his sister called out loudly in return.

'Why not? What's t' keep us here now?'

'Ain't ya forgettin' somethin' we ain't done yet?'

He pondered for a while, felt a bite and tried to hook the fish. The fish got away.

'Well?' she asked.

Frank shook his head and looked at her from under the brim of his hat.

'Nope. Ya got me there. Can't say as I do.'

'Ma an' Pa, of course.' Her own shake of the head demonstrated her disgust. 'You an' me, we haven't settled up with their killers, yet. Now have we?'

'No, but then we ain't likely to. Snakes alive! Be reasonable, Sylvie. If the law can't get a hold of 'em, how in tarnation d'ya expect us to?'

'Maybe the law ain't lookin' hard enough,' she countered. 'Well, the both of us, we can look around real good. And what's more, we've plenty of time t' do it in.'

Resting his pole on a friendly spur of rock, he faced her directly.

'Hey, Sylvie,' he yelled above the roar of the falls, 'hold yer horses for just a cotton-pickin' minute. Ain't ya forgettin' just one little itsy-bitsy detail, eh?'

'And what's that ...' she yelled back in his face. 'Yer beauty-sleep?'

'No it ain't.' His anger was beginning to show. 'While we're lookin' for the killers ... the law's gonna be out lookin' for us.'

'So what? You scared of the law?'

'Course I ain't. But I wasn't born stubborn-stupid neither. I just know, if we're getting ourselves strung up, we ain't never goin' to get our revenge for Ma an' Pa, are we?'

She grimaced and thought awhile. Then she grinned and beckoned him closer, to speak in his ear.

'I guess you've just hooked a fish.'

'What makes ya think that?'

'One's just pulled your fishin' pole over the side.'

Frank and Sylvia stood with bowed heads at the last resting place of their ma and pa. The sun had not yet climbed above the horizon but they still kept a wary eye for the new owners of the holding.

'Amen,' muttered Frank at last and, as his sister repeated the word, he pulled on his hat. They looked sadly at each other, then simultaneously nodded. 'Let's get movin',' he went on. 'I ain't gonna feel safe 'till we've skedaddled right away from this damn awful county.'

As usual they pushed their luck, deciding to take the coach road again. Once more, with their horses tied to the back of the buggy, they headed west.

Shortly after noon, they noticed dust above where the road disappeared into the heat haze.

'What ya reckon?' Sylvia frowned.

Frank considered the dust cloud for a while before committing himself.

'Could be a small herd, but for my money, I'd say it's a stage coach.'

She sat up and faced him, her eyes bright with expectation.

'A stage?' She patted her thigh where the derringer was concealed. 'If it is, let's have us some fun, eh?'

'Not on your life.' Frank glared at her. 'Are ya crazy? We're tryin' t' get away from trouble, not look for more.'

'Oh, Frank … I'm bored out of my hide.'

'Then ya'll stay bored. We ain't riskin' anythin' else. And certainly not just for laughs.'

His conjecture proved to be right. After another mile a stagecoach emerged from the trembling haze, dragging a billowing swirl of dust in its wake. Quickly closing the distance and rocking wildly, the Concord rattled past them. Its driver gave a friendly wave, but the guard merely scowled, and standing precariously, trained his twelve-gauge on them until they were left behind, well out of range.

'The fella ridin' shot-gun wasn't takin' chances. He wouldn't have been so easy t' take.'

'How'd ya know?' she sneered huffily. 'You were too yella t' try.'

'Sylvie … are ya blind or somethin'? He had that scattergun trained on us right from the moment we came into view, 'til we were well past an' out of range.'

'Huh!' Tight-lipped, she stared ahead into the dust left by the stage.

Frank shrugged, accepting his sister's mood as normal.

'Huh, yourself,' he grunted then settled back into the seat, tipped his hat over his face and closed his eyes.

Later in the day, after the stage had rumbled into Yellow Rock, one of the passengers hurried off to speak to the sheriff.

'Of course I'm sure it's them, Sheriff. Hell, I saw 'em before. I'd recognize 'em anywhere. The last time, the gal, she was this close to me.' He held his hands about a foot apart. 'Well, are you goin' t' do somethin' about it?'

The sheriff stared thoughtfully up at the flushed face of the agitated drummer standing in front of his desk. He leaned back and clasped his hands behind his head.

'You sure?'

'Of course I'm sure,' the drummer snapped back. 'Why else would I come in here? You think I've nothin' else better to do, eh?'

'You ever wear eye-glasses, mister?'

'No, and I got all my teeth and I ain't deaf, neither.'

The sheriff was unimpressed. He unclasped his hands, swivelled his chair, and pointed at a notice on the wall to his right.

'Read that out loud for me, will ya?'

Exasperated, the drummer did so, then whirled round on the lawman.

'Well, have I passed?' he snarled.

The sour-faced sheriff ignored the remark and strolled over to read the notice in silence.

'Yep,' he admitted at last. 'That's what it says all right.'

'Do you give me a certificate, or do ya need another eyewitness' to back me up?'

'Hold your horses, mister. I believe ya, but it's my duty to make sure before I fork out county money on raisin' a posse.' Opening a drawer, he took out his gunbelt and yelled through to the cell block out back. 'Clem!'

'Yeah, Sheriff?'

'Get up off yer lazy arse an' come in here. Get the boys t'gether. Tell 'em we've work t' do.'

'Hey, Sheriff,' the drummer broke in. 'If there's any reward …?'

'There ain't.'

'Well, if you find a fancy gold watch and chain on 'em, take a good look. You'll see my initials engraved inside the case, by the winder.'

Frank wound his watch and held it to his ear as he did every night before turning in.

'Checked the horses?' Sylvia asked, in the same way her ma had always asked pa about the chores. 'We don't want 'em wanderin' off when we might be needin' to make a dash for it.'

Frank laughed.

'Who's goin' to come lookin' for us up here when there's miles of good road down below in the valley? From up here ya can see anybody on the road long before they can see us.'

'That why yer lettin' that fire smoke like a chimney?'

She was right. It didn't make sense to advertise their presence. Grudgingly, he raked the smouldering sapwood aside and damped it down with the coffee dregs.

'You put that on,' he challenged.

'That ain't right an' ya know it.' She started to plait her hair and, as she did so, looked east and to the road below. 'Frank … look!'

Her tone was so urgent that he was alongside

her in a second, screwing his eyes up to peer into the gathering gloom.

'That's a posse, or my name ain't Frank Dobson.'

'Look at 'em. They're turnin' off the road, right where we did.'

'Yeah, they're trailin' us real good. If the dark don't slow 'em down, they'll be here in less than an hour.'

He made the decision, scraped earth over the fire and began to don the rest of his clothes.

'Are you stupid? Come on, let's high-tail it out of here. They ain't comin' to make no social call.'

She hurried to load the buggy, but he stopped her.

'Leave the buggy, it'll slow us down. It's best if we stay up in the hills. Riding horseback'll be easier among the rocks than pickin' a path to move the rig around.'

'There's no doubt about it, Frank,' she pointed out as they mounted up minutes later. 'You're right, they are lookin' for us.'

'I'm always right.' With that remark, he reined his steed and moved out past the abandoned buggy.

Sylvia giggled as she drew alongside him.

'Ain't this excitin'?' she blurted out.

'I can live without it.'

'Come mornin', if they're still doggin' us, I'm gonna try me this newfangled rifle.' She leaned forward and felt at the butt of the carbine in its saddle holster. 'I bet it knocks 'em down like apples off a tree.'

EIGHT

'It's them all right.' The sheriff from Yellow Rock picked up a charred stick and scraped away soil from the fire. Immediately a flame broke through. He grinned wryly. 'They've got wind of us and must've lit out of here like hell was after 'em.'

'We goin' on now?' a member of the posse asked.

The lawman looked about him and shook his head. 'Too dark. Don't see any reason to risk breakin' our horses' legs scramblin' around these hills in the dark.' He lit a part-smoked cigar then leaned his back against the buggy. 'No, we'll grab us some sleep, and then start off fresh, first thing.' He blew a smoke ring. 'Let the young fools tire themselves out if they want to. They'll make my job all the easier.'

Round about eleven o'clock on that same night, Frank's horse slipped on a rock and took a tumble down a crumbling bank. Frank fell clear but skinned his face and bruised a knee. When the horse got to its feet it was lame.

'Told ya it was too darned dark to press on like

we've been doin',' Sylvia grumbled. 'This was bound t' happen sooner or later.'

'Quit yer moanin', will ya?' He loosened the cinch and dragged the saddle from the injured animal's back. 'It ain't so bad. I'll saddle up the buggy horse.'

Two minutes later he hurt his left elbow and bust his nose. The buggy horse, never broken and used for riding, had vigorously bucked him from its back.

'It ain't s' bad,' she scoffed, aping his manner of speech. 'I'll saddle up the buggy horse.' Then she laughed.

Holding his left elbow, his face twisted in pain and humiliation, he limped after the reluctant steed and with difficulty retrieved his saddle.

'Well!' he yelled at her, 'don't just sit there like ya was God Almighty. Give me a hand, will ya?'

'Ya ain't ridin' my horse,' she informed him flatly just as the moon broke through the layer of scudding clouds.

'I ain't intendin' to. I'll take the old hay-burner.'

Abandoning both the cripple and the buggy horse, they let them roam free to take their chances. Unable to carry most of their clothes and equipment, they tossed it into a dried-out gulch, but retained the guns and ammunition.

The pack horse was more docile and made no objection when Frank opted to ride him. However, he soon started to moan.

'It's like sittin' astride a barrel, and he rides like a rockin'-horse.'

Sylvia, riding along behind him, laughed again, enjoying her brother's minor discomfort.

'Yer horse is cow-hocked and you're gonna be bow-legged. What a fine pair you'll make.'

When dawn finally broke they were still surrounded by rock-strewn hills.

'Any idea where we are?' she yawned.

'Nope. No idea at all.'

'How far would ya say we've come, since last night?'

Frank twisted round to peer at the hills behind them, studied them for a moment, then shrugged.

'Who knows? Maybe ten miles … maybe fifteen, but no more.'

'How's yer arm and knee?' Sylvia asked. She pointed at his scraped face. 'Yer nose don't look too bad.'

'My knee's stiff as a coffin lid and my elbow, well, that's hurtin' real bad when I move it.'

'Well, don't move it,' Sylvia stated, as always, assuming that things she didn't understand, were simple. 'It can't be so bad if ya can actually move it. Can it?'

They stopped at a water-hole to rest the horses for an hour, to drink coffee and to see to their needs.

'I can't ride that old hay-bag much further,' Frank stated bluntly. 'We're goin' to have to call in some place and buy a decent animal.'

'Buy?' She raised her eyebrows. 'Why buy?'

'Because it's less risky that way. They hang folks for stealin' horses, in case ya didn't know.'

'They hang people for shootin' preachers full of holes ... but that didn't stop ya, did it?'

'We're gonna buy a horse and that's that!'

'Huh!' Sylvia went into a sulk again.

'How much cash have we got ... eh?'

'You're so darned clever ... go see for yourself.'

He limped stiffly over to the horses and began to search the saddle-bags. Then he called out again.

'All right, smart-arse, where've ya put it?'

'Wrapped up in the flour sack, of course. Same as always.'

'Well, there ain't no flour sack here that I can see.'

'Well, lookee here, Sheriff,' one of the posse called out from the bottom of the gulch.

The sheriff gazed down.

'Yeah, Bart, what's that ya got?'

'A flour sack, an' it's got a whole heap of spendin' money inside.'

'Was it hidden?'

'No, it was on the ground, along with the rest of the stuff they'd throwed down.'

'Bring it up here.'

'Hell, Sheriff, these are abandoned goods. I found that money fair an' square.'

'Bring it up.' There was an edge to his voice. 'That money don't belong to nobody 'ceptin' the folks who got robbed on the stage. And that's who's goin' t' get it.'

The half-breed tracker came back from his scouting.

'What ya find out, Joe?' the sheriff asked. 'Anythin' new?'

'Yes, boss. They only use two horses now.'

'Two? What happened t' the others?'

'Let loose. Go that way. One lame.' He extended his arm. 'Riders move slowly that way ... west.'

'So, that's why they've dumped all that stuff. The going's getting too tough for them. They're tired and've started makin' mistakes.'

'Mistakes?' Bart asked as he came up over the top of the gulch side. 'What mistakes?'

'The money, for one. If they'd had their wits about them, they'd never have thrown that away.' The sheriff's grin broadened. 'Money buys all sorts of things when someone's on the run. Without it, an outlaw's usually forced to reveal himself by havin' to take stupid chances.'

'I do good, boss?' Joe asked, encouraged by the lawman's grin.

The sheriff rubbed his palms together.

'You bet ya did.' He slapped the breed on the back. 'Joe, you've done real good. We can't be as far behind them pesky outlaws as I thought.'

Walking tall, he shouted an order.

'Mount up, men ... let's get after them dang-blasted killers and have done with it.'

'The horses in that corral, they ain't for ridin',' Frank whispered. They were hiding behind the woodpile by the side of a hay barn. 'Look out there. Out in front of the main buildin'. See them wheel tracks? This place ain't a ranch. It's a relay station for a stage line.'

'Well, the way I look at things, horses are horses, they'll just have t' do. Anythin's got to be better than that useless critter you've been a-ridin'. Hell, Frank, I've seen dyin' snails that can gallop faster than he can.'

'Shh!' he hissed, pulling her back behind the logs. 'An old-timer … just come out the privy, yonder.'

They watched the old man finish fastening his belt before taking out his pocket watch and checking the time. He looked down the road, shielding his eyes from the sun with both hands. Then, he wandered back into the main building.

'Must be a stage due soon.'

'I know that. I saw what he did,' Sylvia snapped. 'To hear you talk, anyone'd think I'm stupid or somethin'.'

Her brother did not answer. He was too busy gazing down to where the heat shimmered above the road.

'Looks like it's comin' all right. See that dust?' He shaded his eyes and after a while exclaimed. 'Yeah that's it. That's….' He stopped speaking and peered harder. 'Hell, no. It looks like the posse.'

'We can't make a run for it,' Sylvia cried out. 'The horses are plum tuckered out. Besides, the land around here's too open and flat. We'd be seen.'

'Well, we ain't gonna give ourselves up, I'll tell ya that much for nothin'. Come on.'

Keeping low, forgetting the pain of his bruised

knee and swollen elbow, Frank moved back to their mounts, his sister following closely.

'Get them saddles off,' Frank commanded. 'And be quick. We've got t' hide these where they won't give us away.'

She looked around frantically.

'There ain't no such place.'

'Trust me,' he winked. 'I've got it all worked out.'

Minutes later, with their saddles hidden in the woodpile, and their mounts mixed with the other horses in the corral, they took their weapons and went to the barn. There, they climbed the ladder up to the single-span roof, and pressed their bodies as flat as possible to the sun-warmed shingles, hoping for the best.

Peeping down over the edge, and filled with trepidation, they watched the riders draw nearer. Eight of them wheeled in from the road, through the open gateway, pounding into the front yard of the relay station like a charging troop of cavalry.

The riders split up. Five rode straight into the hay barn. The others dismounted and hurried inside the main building. There were shouts, then suddenly a couple of muffled shots. The shouting stopped abruptly. Immediately after, the men who had ridden into the barn, ran across to join the others inside the office and living quarters of the station attendant.

'Somethin's goin' on, Sylvie?' Frank whispered. 'That don't seem like no posse t' me.'

'To me neither.'

All went quiet. After a few minutes Sylvia nudged Frank.

'Look along the road. It's the stage.'

'You understand what's happenin', don't ya, Sylvie?'

'Those guys down below. They're bad-guys, outlaws ... same as us. What we gonna do, Frank?'

'Nothin', except stay alive.'

The old-timer walked out and made his way to greet the stagecoach. Only it wasn't the old man but someone else dressed in his clothes. The pretender began to wave as the coach and team rumbled in.

The unsuspecting driver waved back while the guard stowed his shot-gun out of harm's way behind the seat. As the vehicle crunched and slithered to a stop, there was a hail of gunfire and both company men spilled from the driving seat. Together they plunged headlong down to earth, each on his own side of the coach.

The outlaw dressed in the old-timer's clothes stepped up to the coach and waved his pistol at those inside.

Gingerly, the coach doors swung open and frightened passengers called out, waving white handkerchiefs, and pleading for their lives. The rest of the gang showed themselves, laughing and enjoying the ease with which they had acquired so much wealth.

'Jesus, Sylvie,' Frank suddenly gasped. 'It is ... it's them.'

'Who?'

'Them. That gang down there. They're the ones who gunned down Ma an' Pa.'

'They ain't?'

'They is!' His breathing was getting faster.

'Ya sure?'

'I was the one who got a good look at them, wasn't I?'

'Yeah, Frank, of course, but....'

'It's them, I tell ya. It's them!' He rolled on one side and levered a round into his carbine.

A surge of fear washed over her and she put out her hand to restrain him.

'No, Frank. There's too many of 'em.'

'Maybe, but they're out there in the open, with hand guns. We're up here, under cover, out of their range, and we've got rifles!'

Skinny Johnson was busy pistol-whipping a heavy-built and balding man, when the first Winchester barked out. The bullet pierced the brim of his hat, and caught him full in the back of his head. The flattened lead ploughed on through and, as it emerged, scattered the molars of his right-hand jaw like hailstones dashed against the side of the coach.

Before he could drop down to the sun-baked dirt, a second carbine cracked like a giant stockwhip. The upper body of the man clad in the old-timer's clothes twisted sharply and slammed against the open door of the stagecoach. Flopping forward, he left blood and fragments of backbone adhering to the Concord's leather-covered panel.

Uncertain of where the shots were coming from, the outlaws dashed about, seeking whatever cover they could find.

'Get the cash box; grab the money for Christ's sake. Let's get out of here,' yelled Max Boylan, as another of his gang somersaulted and gurgled his last breath only feet away from him.

A dude passenger, grabbing his chance, brought out a Remington pocket pistol. He was bringing it up on aim, when Max Boylan spotted him and fanned off a couple of shots from his .45 Army Colt. In an instant, the would-be hero was transformed into a well-dressed hunk of dead meat.

'To hell with the money, Max. Let's clear out before we all catch a bullet,' Patch called across from the safety of the adobe building. 'Skinny's dead, so's Kansas an' his sidekick.'

'Right! Cover me. I'm comin' across.'

While Patch poked his Peacemaker around the corner of the building and blazed away at nothing, Max grasped at the opportunity to save his own hide. Head down, crouching low, his heart pounding fit to burst, he ran. Wildly, zig-zagging every yard or two, he weaved through the volley of near-misses.

Another yard and he would have made it unscathed. He felt a scorching pain high up, on his back, close to his right shoulder. The unexpectedness of the wound caused him to cry out, before he lurched and fell into the safety afforded by the wall.

'Holy shit!'

'You hit bad?' Patch knelt down and began to examine the wound.

'Don't know,' Max gasped. 'I ain't never stopped a bullet before.'

Patch chortled and slapped the injured man soundly on the back.

'Well, you ain't stopped one again. Ya lucky bastard, that ain't but a scratch.'

'A scratch?'

'Sure, that's all. You've lost a piece of shirt and a thin strip of skin.' Patch began to laugh. 'Hell,' he continued, 'that bullet was only bein' friendly. It hardly stopped by long enough t' say how-do.'

On the roof of the hay barn, Sylvia and Frank had grown confident of their invincibility. Cool as spring melt-water, they snapped off shot after shot, pinning the outlaws down, giving them no opportunity to fire back with any hope of scoring a hit.

During a lull in the shooting, while Frank was thumbing cartridges into the magazine of his carbine, Sylvia heard the sound of a hammer being drawn back to full cock. The crisp, clear sound came from close behind them.

Rolling onto her back and glancing past her feet, she gaped in disbelief. An outlaw stood on the ladder, waist-high above the edge of the roof.

'Frank!' Her scream was high-pitched and filled with fear.

With the instinctive reactions of a wildcat,

Frank rolled over, along the roof and further from Sylvia. He was already bringing his rifle to bear when the outlaw fired.

Due to the shallow angle offered to the gunman, the hot lead penetrated high in Frank's right chest, drilled through his shoulder blade and left his body, to ricochet off the edge of the roof with a lazy whine.

With both eyes opened wide, Sylvia aimed her Winchester between her feet. The assassin drew a bead on her. She squeezed the trigger. Like a live creature, the butt kicked against her grasp, and the muzzle spewed out death.

The soft lead .44 slug struck him high up, smashing the bone and glancing up over the centre of his forehead. It flattened out and lifted his scalp as neatly as any redskin. His arms jerked up and out, casting his gun away in a wide arc as he fell slowly back. Then a second shot blasted from the carbine, to help him on his way, and he disappeared from view.

'Frank … Frank!' Sylvia discarded the carbine and knelt beside her ashen-faced brother. 'Frank?'

To her relief he opened his eyes, noticed her brimming tears, and whispered to her.

'Sylvie … my chest … an' my shoulder. Jesus, it hurts.'

'I'll get a doctor,' she blurted out, the shock realization of what could have happened, still held her in its fearful grip. 'I'll….'

He had to grin.

'Ya ain't ever gonna change, are ya? Calm down,

I'm gonna be fine. We've got to get away from here first. That's the main thing.'

With difficulty, and her help, he eased himself over on to his side. Now he could keep an eye on what was happening by the stagecoach, and the area in front of the barn.

'Can't see any of 'em,' she murmured, fighting to remain calm.

'Me neither.' He winced as the fire of pain in his wound flared up. He gasped. 'Wish I knew what they're intendin' t' do.'

Removing his bandanna, she ripped open his shirt and inspected the wound.

'It ain't bleedin s' much as I thought. And the hole's not so big. Maybe if I can plug it with this....' She used her teeth and tore the bandanna, then as gently as she was able, plugged the entry hole.

Before finishing her doctoring, she glanced at the scene around. Her heart missed a beat.

'Look, back there ...' Sylvia urged. 'See what's a-comin' like a bat out of hell, along the road.' Her shoulders sagged and she sighed. 'It's that damned posse again.'

'Yeah, like a hungry dog gnawin' away at a big old bone.' Frank heaved a disappointed sigh of resignation and let his face rest on the warm roof. 'I reckon that sheriff's kinda single-minded.' He shut his eyes tight and winced again. 'Sorry, Sylvie.' A wan smile twisted the ends of his lips. 'Looks as though this time we've been dealt a losin' hand. Don't it?'

NINE

The sudden frantic drumming of hooves, accompanied by the random firing of hand guns, told Frank and Sylvia that the situation had changed.

Down by the stagecoach the stranded passengers ran around in utter confusion, either shouting or screaming until, one by one, they finally dived for cover.

Back along the stage road, but still a good distance away, the posse, no doubt spurred on by the sound of gunfire, kicked up more dust as they increased speed.

'I just don't believe it,' Frank murmured, forcing himself into a sitting position and gazing as if in some kind of dream.

'Me neither.' Totally awed, Sylvia watched open-mouthed as the outlaws galloped their mounts out through the front gateway of the relay station. Without bothering to look back, the remains of the gang stampeded across the stage-trail. Like well-aimed arrows, they headed for the distant hills.

Realizing their ordeal was over, the passengers swarmed from their hiding places to watch the departing bandits, and began to cheer. Someone pointed to the fast-approaching posse and, to a man, they rushed out to greet them. Their cheering increased in volume as they enthusiastically urged the posse on, and directed them after the retreating outlaws.

To the utmost delight of the pair on the roof, the posse changed direction and hightailed it after the gang.

'Well I'll be....' Frank forced a grin as he mustered the strength to stand. 'I thought we were gonners for sure.'

'We still could be, if we don't mount up and hit the trail before the sheriff and his boys come back,' his sister reminded him. She held out a hand to steady him as they made their way down the sloping roof to the ladder. 'Take it easy,' she joked. 'I'd hate ya t' break yer neck without a rope round it.'

'Hey, you fellas ... oops, sorry ma'am, didn't realize one of you was a gal. Are you both OK?' They recognized the speaker on the ground beside the ladder as one of the passengers. He was smiling up, real friendly like, and holding his hands out ready to help.

'He's been shot in his shoulder,' Sylvia explained, quick to take advantage of the situation. 'I'll have to get him to a doctor, he needs fixin' up.'

'It ain't nothin' at all, mister,' announced

Frank, ashen-faced and wincing with every step he took. 'Why don't you take charge of the passengers ... take 'em inside for a rest and maybe rustle up some hot coffee to ease everyone's nerves, eh?'

'That sounds good to me,' the passenger nodded. 'But how about you two?'

'Oh we've got a job t' do. We'll just have to stick by company rules and do our duty.' Frank managed a wry grin. 'We gotta take care of the stage first.'

'What's your name, young fella-me-lad? You and this young lady, you saved all our hides today.'

'The name's Frank Dobson ... my sister, Sylvia. What we did was nothin'. It's what we're paid t' do.'

'Remarkable!' The dude smiled in wonder and admiration. 'You're real heroes, and I'm going to see the stage company gets a glowing report on you both. Yes sir. You and your sister are both credits to this country and the younger generation.'

'Thanks. We sure try, sir,' Sylvia smiled shyly. 'Now, if you'll take the others inside, we can do our job.'

Unhitching the team, they led them into the corral while the passengers were collected together and taken indoors.

'Look over there, at the hitchin-rail.'

'Yeah I've already seen 'em, Frank. Two good horses already saddled and beggin' t' be took.'

'Go get 'em.' He grinned as he fastened the corral gate. 'But be nice an' casual, like yer just gettin' things back the way they should be.'

'And what'll you be doin' ... just watchin' me?' she asked huffily, suspecting she was doing more than her share, as usual.

'I'll be workin' on the stage as company rules demand.' He winked. 'Didn't ya hear me tell that fine upstandin' citizen that? And if he looks out of a window, ain't that what he expects us to be a-doin'? Well, ain't it?'

She stared at him, suspicious, wondering what game he was playing.

'We're gonna be caught if we don't move on out of here good an' fast.'

'No we ain't. That posse'll be miles away by now. So go an' get them horses, like you've been told. Be quick, but try not t' be noticed.'

As Sylvia brought the horses around to where he was standing at the rear of the coach, she discovered him with an iron-bound and locked cashbox, held by the handle and swinging at his side.

'Told ya I was workin', didn't I? Well. I've just been pickin' up our due wages from the company.'

Hefting it up with one hand, he held it while she secured it to the rear of his saddle by the bedroll straps. Then, using the boot of the stagecoach as a mounting block, he swung his leg across the saddle.

'Which way?' she asked, gathering the reins neatly in her left hand.

'The sheriff and his boys went that way. And we ain't chasin' them!' Frank answered with a pained expression. Turning in the saddle he nodded in the opposite direction. 'For my money, that trail's favourite.'

Gently, without fuss or hurry, they walked their newly acquired mounts away from the main building, then on past the barn and the outlaw Sylvia had shot off the ladder.

'Easy!' Frank boasted as he winked happily at her. 'The Dobson gang does it again.'

Confident no one had seen them leaving, they set off at a steady canter.

'We'll not be seein' that place again in a hurry,' Sylvia said after a final glance behind. 'Now what we need is to find a saw-bones, for that shoulder of yours.'

'I sure wish we still had that buggy,' Frank admitted some hours later. 'I don't feel good.'

'Let's stop. Have a break, eh?'

'No. Stoppin' won't find us a doc, will it?'

'And it won't kill the horses, either,' she snapped back. 'Just half an hour. Enough to have a drink and a mess o' beans.'

She won the day.

'Let's open the box,' she suggested, as he scraped the last of the beans from his plate with his knife.

'OK ... bring it here.'

'I'm all excited. What d'ya think's inside?' she asked, setting it down where he lounged.

'Well it ain't likely t' be last week's dirty laundry, that's for sure.' Taking his Adams he fired at the top of the padlock. The buckled lock sprang open, and eagerly he clawed at the lid.

His jaw dropped, and so did hers. For ages they held their breaths, staring at the contents. She was the first to utter a word.

'Oooh!'

'Jesus!' Frank whispered. 'Oh sweet, sweet Jesus.'

'Frank … it's packed.' Reaching slowly into the box, she let her trembling fingers stroke the money as though to convince herself it was real. She heaved a loud shuddering sigh. 'There must be … hundreds.'

'No,' he whispered. 'Thousands!' Picking up a bundle of new ten-dollar bills, he riffled the crisp edges with his thumb. 'See how thick these are.' In a trance he lifted his head. Their eyes crinkled at the sides as they smiled. In a voice brimming with emotion, he gasped, 'Sylvie … you an me … we're rich!'

Buoyed up by the winning hand of lady-luck, they pressed on, steadily putting more miles between them and the resolute sheriff of Yellow Rock.

The sun was casting longer shadows behind them as they halted at the edge of a canyon. This great gouge out of the land blocked their trail with unclimbable vertical cliffs which furrowed into the prairie as far as they could see in either direction.

'We could've done without this,' Frank sighed as he stared down at the flowing ribbon of water far below. 'Which way now? That's the big question.'

'North,' she said briskly, eager to have her say in the running of things.

'Yeah, why not. It feels right t' me. But I sure wish we knew where we're headin' for.'

Reining their mounts to the right they followed the rock-strewn edge of the chasm. At least, heading north enabled them to turn dazzled and watering eyes from the direct rays of the late afternoon sun.

The wound in Frank's shoulder had begun to weep past the bandanna plugs. He could feel the blood trickling down his chest and soaking through his shirt into his vest. Besides that, the pain had grown worse and he had begun to sweat much more than was normal.

His sister who had kept a careful eye on him, now rode her animal closer, ready to reach out and prevent him from falling.

'Hold on, Frank, we'll be makin' camp soon.'

He groaned and gasped.

'I need a doc.'

'I know, but there ain't one handy, and we can't stop here.'

Four miles further on, at a point where the canyon narrowed, they came upon a bridge. The dubious contraption consisted of well-weathered fraying rope and logs. The whole thing sagged, swung and creaked alarmingly in the rising evening breeze.

Frank, who had ridden the last two miles with his eyes shut and his chin resting on his chest, raised his head when Sylvia pulled both horses to a stop. He stared in horror.

'Oh no, Sylvie ... there ain't no way I'm goin' to ride across that thing.'

'Of course ya won't,' she conceded, slipping stiff and aching, from her saddle. 'It'd be plum crazy to ride over them roped-on logs.' She gave him a reassuring smile. 'Ya'll walk over, and I'm gonna be right along with ya, t' see you don't step off.'

'No ... no, I couldn't!'

'Ya can.... Yer gonna!' She reached up, gave him a firm yet gentle tug, and when he relented, helped him dismount.

'This pile of kindling'll collapse any minute.' Frank clutched the post at the beginning of the bridge, and held on. 'God alone knows how long it's been slung across there. Just look at it, will ya? It's rotten.'

Boldly she stepped onto the moving log walkway and then faced him. Feet astride, bracing herself, she held out her hands. Beckoning Frank with her waving fingers, she smiled to give him confidence.

'Come on, big brother, hold on t' me.' As he still showed reluctance, her smile died. Taking a step towards him she fastened a firm grip on the arm on his un-injured side, and pulled. 'I ain't gonna let you stay here an' die.'

He stayed put. She heaved harder.

'Now, walk. Ya chicken-livered fool ... walk!'

The bridge rippled as they took each step. It swayed and a wave of movement travelled back and forth along its length. The dust-caked ropes squeaked as they rubbed against the skinned logs, and the sun-split timbers groaned alarmingly under their combined weights. Out of sheer fright, each grabbed at the fraying hand-ropes at the side.

'I can't do it, Sylvie.'

'Ya can.'

'Can't. Ya know how I've always been with heights.'

'Just shut yer eyes,' she coaxed. 'I'll guide ya all the way.'

He paid no heed, just stood there, pop-eyed, staring down at the river far below, and frozen as rigid as a dry stick.

'Frank.'

'No.'

Her temper and frustration welled up to replace her own inner fear. She swiped her open palm across his cheek with a crack which echoed along the canyon like a pistol shot. Then she clawed his hand free from the guard rope.

'Damn ya, Frank,' she screamed. 'Come on!'

Her stinging blow did the trick. Shutting his eyes and saying nothing more, he began to walk forward. Slowly, cautiously feeling and testing each log with his foot before permitting his weight to rest on them, he followed. All this time, he held on to his resolute sister, tightly, like she was life itself.

Gradually the far end of the rickety bridge came closer until at last their feet trod on firm ground once more. After she had helped him to a place of shelter behind a group of giant boulders, they lay panting from the effort of their ordeal.

'See?' she said. 'You've made it.'

He made no reply, just lay back, his eyes still closed while his hand tenderly held his wound as he bit his lips to counter the increased pain.

'Now you hold on.' Her words were softer now. 'I'm just goin' back across t' fetch the horses.'

'No, it's too dangerous,' he cautioned, but he was too late. She had already gone.

Across on the far end of the bridge again, Sylvia removed her jacket, and secured it over the eyes of the first horse. Then, conscious of the extra weight of the animal, she stood peering at the makeshift structure, gathering her courage. But she knew there was no other choice. Inhaling deeply, she stepped boldly on, pulling the reluctant and quivering animal after her.

From time to time, logs bent, some splintered a little, and others cracked, threatening to break under the extra load placed upon them. But they held together. Near the middle where the swing was at its greatest, the horse stopped.

'Damned stupid animal,' she began shouting in frustration. Then she softened her voice and coaxed. 'Come along fella. You be real good and I just might find ya some sugar.' Persevering, and continually soothing with her voice, she patted the great arching neck. 'Easy, fella ... easy.'

Gently her other hand pulled on the sweat-soaked cheekstrap, and the frightened horse was persuaded to walk on.

After one more, similar hair-raising journey, the crossing was completed and she set to and made camp.

'Right,' she ordered, easing him into a sitting position by the campfire. 'Let's have that shirt and fancy vest of yours off.' She rested the blade of a knife in the hot embers of the fire. 'We've got t' do somethin' about that wound. If we don't, you'll likely catch lead poisonin' and ya'll be dead as mutton before we find a doctor.'

Frank did not answer. Instead, contorting his face and grunting with the effort, he used the hand on his good side to pull his shirt tails from the waistband of his pants. Carefully, unhooking his watch chain, he unbuttoned his vest, then allowed his sister to help him remove the clothing as painlessly as she could.

By the time she had him ready, rivers of perspiration had carved white maps through the thick coating of trail dust adhering to his face.

'Right-oh, big brother, open yer mouth.' Almost before his lips parted, she had shoved a piece of stick in between his teeth. 'Chew on this, till I'm done with ya.'

His breathing became noisy. His chest began to heave as he watched her go to the fire. She withdrew the blade from the embers. It was cherry-red and spitting out a myriad sparks like miniature shooting stars. Avoiding his eyes, she drew close, her jaw set in grim determination.

Deep creases wrinkled into the skin of his forehead. He bit hard on to the wood and squeezed his eyes shut. A sudden hissing noise was accompanied by a small cloud of smoke which swirled up above the rocks before being dispersed by the evening breeze. There was an instant recognizable smell of roasting meat, and the stick between his teeth snapped under the pressure from his jaws. But apart from a strangled groan, he did not yell out.

Quickly he was pulled forward. Again the smoke and stench of cooking flesh rode on the wind. For the second time, Sylvia applied the hot steel, this time cauterizing the exit-hole in his back left by the departing bullet.

Frank grunted like before, then sagged sideways to rest against a boulder, in a dead faint.

She had almost completed bandaging him when, as pale as chalk, he came round. His words came out in a dry-mouthed whisper.

'How did it go, Sylvie?'

Fondly, she stroked his hair back from his brow and smiled.

'Fine. Ya did well. Real well. I'm proud of ya.'

But he was not listening. He frowned and held his head to one side.

'What's wrong?' she asked, concerned again.

'Did ya hear it?'

'Hear it?' It was her turn to frown. She tensed, straining her ears for some clue.

Frank did not answer. A horse snickered, but it

was not one of their animals. Standing, Sylvia craned her neck and looked over the top of the boulders around them. Immediately the sound of horseshoes walking and clicking on rock came to her from the trail along the far side of the canyon.

She moaned in despair.

'Jesus!'

TEN

Illuminated, blinded by the almost horizontal rays of the sun, hungry and dusty, the members of the posse rode in silence. They were saddle-sore and in need of a rest. Picking their way between scattered rocks and boulders, they moved in a straggling file, following the half-breed tracker.

A couple of hundred yards further on, the breed sat an Indian pony and, head down, worked alone along the rim of the canyon, dogging the Dobsons' trail.

The sheriff from Yellow Rock looked miserable as he slouched in his saddle. His right cheek bulged rosy-red, and he chewed with more care than usual on the new wad of baccy he'd just bitten off.

'Ain't any damn thing gonna go right since I took on this dang-awful job?'

'Hecky me, it ain't your fault, Sheriff,' one of the volunteers said, jumping to the wrong conclusion and kindly attempting to reassure him. 'Plenty of other folk could've made the same mistake as you done ... goin' after the wrong outlaws ... and lettin' the Dobson gang rob the stage.'

'Oh hell, I ain't belly-achin' about them none,' the lawman was quick to correct. 'Two kids out on the prod won't keep me awake at night. No sir, I'll hang 'em sooner or later. It's this dang-awful tooth.' Automatically he tapped the side of his jaw to show where it hurt, and wished he hadn't. 'Jesus, this tooth abscess, it's comin' up like a full growed cactus, bustin' out through my gum. I tell ya, this thing's comin' close t' drivin' me out of my mind.'

'Looks like some kind of bridge up ahead, Sheriff,' a deputy butted in loudly, riding up from behind. 'The breed ... he's wavin' to us.'

The sheriff sat up straight. Bending the left side of his hat's broad brim to shield his eyes, he signalled with an energetic wave, for the tracker to push on.

'He's a good tracker, the breed,' the deputy said with a mixture of jealousy and some admiration. 'I don't know how he does it most of the time.'

'Same way as anybody else who don't know a fish's fart from a gale,' the sheriff snarled. 'That lazy coot just follows the piles o' horse-shit and old cigar butts. He's got to have his nose wedged right up a horse's arse before he knows for certain the horse is there at all.'

'That's their tracker,' Frank pointed out as he and his sister observed the half-breed. They looked out through a tangle of brushwood and long yellowed grass, growing in front of the boulder which concealed them, close to the end of the bridge. From there they had a clear view, along the entire length of its makeshift structure.

'Guess he knows we've crossed over. See, he's signalling back along the trail,' Sylvia said needlessly.

'Yeah,' Frank raised his head a little to see better. 'And that's the Yella Rock sheriff, who's wavin' him on.'

'What'll we do?'

Frank looked pained by such a foolish question. Reaching down he freed the restraining loop of leather from his pistol, and careful not to start his wound bleeding again, unshipped the Adams.

'I'll tell ya what I'm gonna do,' he informed her, grinning. 'I'm goin' to plug any bastard who's stupid enough to set foot on that bridge.'

'You can't ... not like that, Frank, yer wounded bad.'

'I ain't gonna be choppin' down trees,' he sneered. 'Only men.'

'But, Frank, be reasonable. We can't shoot 'em all. There's too many of 'em,' she argued back in her usual manner.

'We got enough bullets, ain't we? Besides, they're not gonna charge in a bunch. Not across a narrow bridge like that,' he announced with all the confidence of his youth. 'Remember what it said in Momma's Bible ... about that strong fella, with the long hair?'

She frowned.

'Ya mean, Samson?'

'Yeah, him. Well, this Samson guy, was in a tight corner, all on his ownsome. He stood in a narrow cleft, and held off an army with nothin' more than the jaw-bone of an ass.'

'But he was a fit man,' she retorted. 'And he didn't have a bullet-hole all the way through his shoulder.'

'No ... but then he never had no gun, neither. Did he?'

With a sudden clatter of hooves, the breed, either through lack of imagination or sheer laziness, rode his pinto directly on to the bridge. He had almost reached the half-way mark when Frank fired.

The Indian pinto tumbled to its knees and screamed in pain and fear. Rolling over, its legs thrashed wildly, setting the whole structure creaking and snaking from one side of the canyon to the other. Then, still kicking and screaming, it rolled out between the support ropes at the north side of the bridge and fell from sight.

On the opposite side, the breed, saved from the same death plunge only by his cat-like reactions, clung to the rope hand-rail. Dangling precariously in mid air, his scrawny knees were raised high, displacing his breech-cloth, and showing his naked backside to the world as his moccasined feet scrabbled desperately for a foothold on the logs.

One foot gained a hold, then the other. He hauled himself upright on the outside of the bridge. He was about to move to safety when

Sylvia fired her rifle. The breed arched his back and let go of his handholds. Without a single cry he fell in a graceful backward dive into the chasm.

'Frank, did ya see that? Did ya see that dirty son of a bitch drop off that bridge?' Sylvia laughed. Her eyes sparkled and her cheeks were flushed with the strange excitement of another kill. 'I swear, that breed could've trained t' be an acrobat with a big-time medicine show.'

Shots came, zinging like hornets through the brushwood, snipping off twigs, chipping at the rocks and ricocheting around the outlaws. But the posse, still blinded by the setting sun, could only fire a storm of lead in the hope of scoring lucky hits on unseen targets.

'Get yer stupid head down if ya don't want an extra eye-hole,' Frank warned. 'Damn that lousy Indian pony. I wanted it to stay on the bridge.'

'Maybe ya should've gone out there and told the poor critter exactly what t' do,' his sister sniggered. 'Anyhow, I don't see what difference it'll make. There ain't no one gonna ride it. Certainly not the breed.'

'I wanted that horse to act as a sort of barricade, to stop other horses from comin' on over in a rush.'

Sylvia stared at him incredulously.

'And you … call me stupid?' She stopped speaking and snuggled down further behind her boulder while another tornado of bullets splattered the rocks around them and sang away into the evening light beyond.

She waited for the noise to die.

'Who in the world's gonna be so insane as to try and ride over like that fool breed did? I bet there ain't one o' them fellas over there who'd risk it for a whole extra year's wages.'

Time passed slowly. The sky turned purple and darkness crept over everything. As the temperature dropped, the wind increased and moaned miserably through the canyon. Soon the swaying bridge made enough noise to cover any footsteps.

'I don't like it,' Frank murmured.

'That makes two of us,' Sylvia agreed. 'With all that racket, an' this darkness, the posse could cross any time. We wouldn't know 'til they're right here, a-pokin' us in the eye with their guns.'

'Well, we got t' do somethin' or we'll never get any sleep, I'm tired as a grizzly in late fall, and I need to push on and find a doc.'

Behind the boulders, in the glow from the fire he became aware of her sudden tenseness, then felt her grip his wrist.

'What's wrong?'

'Somebody's on the bridge,' she whispered urgently.

He listened, tutted, then shook his head.

'Yer hearin' things. It's the wind.'

'No, it ain't.' She lifted the Winchester, and slipping the muzzle out through a gap in the rocks, aimed it into the void and waited.

'Well, if yer gonna fire … for Christ's sake, fire,' he grumbled after an inordinate length of time had elapsed. 'You've got my nerves twangin' like a banjo string.'

Hardly had the last word left his mouth when she squeezed the trigger. Her gun belched flame. From near the middle of the span, someone cursed. Another gun flashed as it returned a shot. Sylvia, taking advantage of the gun-flash, fired again. The man on the bridge cried out in pain and his rifle was heard bouncing and clattering on to the roped logs.

Before she had the opportunity to discharge another round his way, the rest of the posse blazed off a hail of bullets. Prudently, both brother and sister ducked back behind cover and reconsidered their position.

'Ya know when ya told me to fire ... back then?' she began. 'Well, it kind of gave me an idea.'

'Well?' he grunted as the firing trailed off.

'Just that ... fire! They can't get over here if we burn the bridge.'

Wasting no time, Sylvia collected enough dried grass and dead branches to do the job. In spite of his pain, Frank insisted on helping her to twist some of the grass into rough ropes to bind the bundles.

Crawling on her belly to the end of the bridge, she carefully placed the bundles of tinder around the support ropes. Her job done, she rejoined her brother, just as the moon decided to slip from behind the clouds.

Secure behind the ring of boulders, Frank had the campfire blazing again with fresh wood he had piled on. Satisfied that all was as planned, he took up a burning brand and threw it like a flaming spear at one of the bundles. It missed, but served to act as a marker for his further attempts.

The sheriff's men, realizing what was happening, were firing again. This time, the increased firelight offered them a narrower target area, their richocheting lead making things more dangerous and difficult for the young outlaws.

Keeping behind cover as much as possible, Frank hurled the burning brands until his sister uttered a delighted yell of triumph.

'Yeah! You've done it, big brother. You've gone an' done it.'

From the safety of their hide, Sylvia and Frank gazed with satisfaction as the flames, fanned by the wind, licked and danced along the dried-out supporting ropes. Soon the fire travelled across to the other side of the canyon and had already ignited the logs.

The left-hand main support rope parted first. As it gave way, the bridge twisted and lurched so that the logs, now well ablaze, hung vertically in a rippling curtain of flame. Then, after quite a while, the right-hand support snapped close to where Sylvia and Frank were watching. A trailing shower of sparks followed the remains of the bridge as it swung down to clatter against the opposite wall of the canyon.

It remained suspended until the consuming fire dismantled it. Then, log by burning log, it finally plunged into the dark depths below.

Ten days after Frank had had his wounds

stitched, he was sitting up in the best room of the smartest hotel in town. As perky as a fighting cock, he tucked into a steak which would have daunted a hungry lion.

'This sure is the life,' he grinned at Sylvia who primped in the mirror at the fancy clothes she'd come in with. 'Money surely does make a difference to what folks think on ya.'

'It sure does,' she answered, twirling in front of him. 'What's the doc have t' say t'day?'

'Told me everythin's fine an' dandy. Said he don't need t' see me no more. So I paid him on the nail, and gave him a little extra for his trouble.' He laughed. 'It made me feel real good. That fella acted so darned surprised and pleased, for a moment I thought the old bastard was gonna kiss me.'

'I like money,' she sighed happily. 'It's so … handy!'

Another month skipped by almost unnoticed. Gradually, their confidence grew. There had been no sign of the sheriff from Yellow Rock, or his posse. Life was good.

Here in the town where they had chosen to linger for a while, the local law officers always tipped their hats politely to them, whenever they passed by on the boardwalks. And shopkeepers welcomed them with open arms.

'I wish Ma and Pa were here, with all the kids,' Sylvia said wistfully as they drove down Main Street in their brand new buggy, loaded with stuff they had collected from the mercantile. 'What a wing-ding of a time we'd all have.' She began to cry. 'It ain't fair.'

'Oh, sweet Jesus,' Frank groaned. 'There ya go again. Never satisfied. Always hankerin' after the impossible then endin' up in stupid tears over it.'

'Yeah, there I go again,' she snapped. 'And so what? I'll keep on doin' just that.' She sniffed loudly several times, and dabbed at her eyes. 'Ya know we still haven't settled up with their killers, and ya made a sacred promise, so don't go tryin' t' deny it.'

'I ain't denyin' no such thing. And I know I've not settled up with all of 'em, but I will,' he confirmed. 'But, hell, Sylvie, we've accounted for some of 'em. How about that two-faced Bible-thumpin' preacher? He ain't gonna let any more little kids go up in flames, now is he?'

'No, but …' she began but was interrupted by him again.

'And there's only two of the gunhands who murdered our folks still livin', ain't there?' he persisted. 'The one they call Max Boylan, an' the other with the eye-patch. Be reasonable, Sylvie. We can't say for sure if they're still alive or not.'

'Ya saw 'em, didn't ya?'

'Yeah, ya know I did … but not after that posse chased after 'em, that time at the stage relay station.'

Frank's words trailed off. He could tell his sister was no longer listening. She had a familiar, far-away look in her glazed eyes and she stood with her head tilted to one side.

'Frank,' she began, thoughtfully, 'them lawyer fellas ... they ain't allowed to break a client's confidence, are they, eh?' Galvanized into action, she spun round to face him and her eyes stared right into his. 'Well, that right, or ain't it?'

Sensing more trouble on the way, he thought carefully before making a reply.

'That's what I've heard. Don't know for certain if it's true or not.' Deeply suspicious of her motives, he peered back through half-closed eyes. 'Why ya wanna know? Sylvie, what've ya got in mind?'

They stood outside the building with the highly polished brass plate screwed to the door. Engraved was the legend *Jason M Clintock Jr, Attorney at Law*.

'I wish I was sure about this,' Frank grumbled. 'Ya really want t' go through with it?'

'We've an appointment. I'm here ain't I?' She pushed past him, opened the door with a flourish and walked in leaving him to follow.

Jason Clintock extended his hand to greet them like long-lost friends. He was not as they had imagined him. Instead of a wizened old man, he was tall, good looking and not more than thirty. He wore a neat business suit and an engaging smile.

'Ah, Mr and Miss Dobson,' he announced in a deep cultured voice. 'Most people call me JC.' He ushered them on to horsehair-stuffed chairs, carefully arranged in front of his impressive polished desk. 'Please, make yourselves comfortable then tell me what I can do for you?'

'First, Mr ... er ...' Frank began.

'Please, JC.' The lawyer smiled, and took his seat, looking interested.

'All right, JC. Is it right that any mortal thing we say to you is private? I mean, you won't tell a soul anythin' we don't want ya to?'

'That is perfectly true. What goes on between an attorney and his client is sacrosanct.'

'No matter what?' Sylvia piped up. 'Not even to a sheriff or anyone like that?'

'Not even to the President himself,' Clintock affirmed. 'It doesn't matter if you tell me you've had your hand in the cookie jar, or you've poisoned your grandmother. Everything remains strictly between ourselves.'

Frank turned to Sylvia and raised his eyebrows in question. She paused for a short while, then nodded.

'We, that's my sister an' me, we want to offer a reward.'

It was the lawyer's turn to raise his eyebrows.

'A reward? A reward for what, and for how much?'

'A thousand dollars.' Sylvia stood up and leaned forward with both of her hands resting on the edge of the desk. 'For the whereabouts of the killers of our ma and pa. Is that enough, mister? We can make it more if we have to.'

'Enough?' He was taken aback. 'Judas himself only received thirty pieces of silver.' He gestured with his hands. 'A thousand dollars ... that is a substantial sum, ma'am. To my mind it's more than adequate.' JC indicated her chair again. 'Please, sit and relax.' He picked up a small brass bell from his desk. 'Tea or coffee,' he suggested.

'Coffee'll do fine, JC,' Frank told him. 'For both of us.'

The bell tinkled and when a woman opened the office door, Clintock gave the order and waited until the door had closed again.

'Right-oh. Suppose you tell me all about it, from the beginning.'

'Well,' Frank commented, 'them reward posters JC sent out to all the towns around should work like a charm. Ya know, he seems to be real keen on gettin' results.' He pulled up the buggy, a mile downriver outside of town, where they always carried out their target practice. 'Seems a lot keener now than he did on that first day, when we met in his office.'

'I know,' Sylvia answered coyly. 'When I met him in the street the other day ... mentioned I'd make it worth his while, to find that Max Boylan, quick, along with his one-eyed pal. Just t' get the business over an done with.'

He stopped, one foot on the ground as he dismounted from the vehicle, and doubt showed clearly on his brow.

'What ya mean, *you'd make it worth his while?* Hey, you ain't been doin' anythin' stupid, have ya?'

'That's a laugh. Chance would be a fine thing. You're worse than Ma an' Pa ever were. Ya never leave me alone long enough to do anythin' ... even if I wanted to.' Nimbly she jumped down with a Winchester clutched in her hand. 'Sometimes I feel I'd have more freedom inside a prison.'

'I'm yer brother. I'm responsible for ya,' he yelled, angered by her sudden revelation. 'You're all the kin I got left in the whole damned world.' Stomping after her he caught hold of her shoulder and spun her round to face him. 'Hey, I'm talkin' t' you.'

'Huh! That's you all over. Always shootin' yer big mouth off and sayin' what's best for me. Look at me. Ain't ya noticed? I'm full growed. I got feelin's the same as any other woman. I want me a husband and kids, the same as Ma had. I need a proper home. I want t'live like normal folks.'

With that outburst over, she pulled away from him and stomped over to the fallen tree on the river-bank, to set up the usual row of small stones to use as targets. Slowly he wandered along after her, bewildered by the unexpectedness of this turn of events.

'Why didn't ya say?' he said, picking up more small rocks to add to the line-up.

'Because you'd never listen. You've always known best ... or thought ya did.'

'Ya wanna go away ... leave me?'

Sylvia shook her head.

'No, not like that. We could buy a farm or even a horse ranch maybe. Somethin' like that. We could all live there and share life together.'

'All? I don't understand yer figurin'.'

'We could get married.'

He burst out laughing.

'Don't be stupid. Close kin can't wed,' he informed her when he had calmed down a little.

'I didn't mean you an' me … I meant we could marry other folks we might come across.'

'No. Yer too dang young.' This time his tone was authoritative.

'No, I ain't! Ma was rockin' you in the cradle when she was my age. Her an Pa got themselves hitched a whole year before that.'

'Well you can forget it. Yer doin' fine as ya are. As for me gettin' hitched to a woman, I ain't gettin' wed for years yet.'

'Well that's up to you,' she announced with a toss of her head. 'But me, I've got a hankerin'. I've made up my mind t' start lookin', from this day on.'

They had endured two days of silent sulking, when a message came from Jason Clintock. It was delivered by hand at the hotel.

Frank was the first to speak.

'It's from JC. Says he wants t' see us right away, Sylvie.'

'Oh?' She pretended not to care.

Moving closer than he had been since the row, he spoke as if nothing had happened.

'Look.' He held out the paper to her and tapped it meaningfully with his crooked finger. 'It's about that reward idea of yours.'

'Is it?' She craned her neck, attempting to read the writing.

But he deliberately withdrew it again, teasing her, and laughing, holding it out of her reach as she followed him around the room.

'Come on,' she pleaded, 'tell me what it says.'

His words were deliberately casual.

'There's good news.'

ELEVEN

'Come in, come in.' JC grinned fit to split his face in two. 'Have I got news for you.' He took up a letter from his desk and waved it excitedly.

'You've a result from the posters,' Sylvia blurted out hopefully. 'Someone knows where the killers are holed-up?'

'Better than that. Max Boylan and the one they call Patch … they're already in jail, waiting to go on trial tomorrow.'

'Where?' Frank demanded. 'Who's that letter from?'

'Yellow Rock, and it's genuine,' JC answered. 'It's from the sheriff there. He's claiming the reward you've offered.'

'The sheriff? Are you sure?' Sylvia was doubtful.

The attorney frowned and slapped the paper with the back of his hand.

'It's written on official paper from the sheriff's office. It gives details about the charges, the circuit judge and the time of the trial. According to this letter, the case is already cut and dried. They're going to hang for what they did. Even so, we can easily check up on all the facts. You don't have to worry. I'll make sure of everything before I hand over your money.'

'We don't give two hoots for the money,' Frank snapped. 'We trust ya, but don't want any slip-ups. We expect everythin' to be right, that's all.'

'Of course.' Clintock shrugged and swiftly passed the letter over the desk for Frank to read. At the same time he attempted to divert a little.

'Well, that's a coincidence isn't it?' he declared. 'Those scoundrels, after all this time, being tried so close to where they committed the crime.'

There was no immediate comment. He looked embarrassed.

'Aren't you pleased?'

Brother and sister looked into each other's eyes, and a barely perceptible signal passed between them. Then, pale-faced, Sylvia smiled back at the attorney.

'Of course we're pleased. In fact, we're delighted to be having such quick results, ain't we, Frank?'

'Oh, yeah, sure,' Frank stammered, worried by the thoughts of the Yellow Rock sheriff. As if to back her up, he said, 'We'd go to the trial ourselves but as it's all set for tomorrow, even if we rode hard all day and through the night, we couldn't make it in time. They'll be hung before we can get there.'

'Oh, that's no problem. We can go today, by the afternoon train,' he persisted.

'There ain't no rail line been laid to Yella Rock,' Frank countered gratefully.

'Yes, I know that,' JC agreed. 'But the line from

here goes to within easy reach. We can go most of the way by train, then travel by the regular stage for the final six miles.'

'Oh ... that's fine.' Frank gave a sickly grin.

'Can't wait,' added Sylvie.

'Of course, I shall be going too,' JC announced. 'I'll need to take the reward money along and, if all the conditions have been met, pay it out as promised. But I can't believe that the letter's a foolish hoax. And from my point of view, it's a new circuit judge. I'd like to study how he handles the trial. So why not make a party of it?' He looked hopefully from one to the other. 'Agreed?'

Back in the hotel, as they packed for the journey, Frank fumed.

'I hate bein' rushed. If we ain't careful, it's us who'll be hangin' like crow-bait alongside them outlaws.' He banged his fist on the table. 'Damn that sheriff. Why did it have to be him?'

'We couldn't exactly refuse to go,' Sylvia reasoned. 'It would seem downright suspicious. Fancy offerin' a reward then not showin' an interest in the trial or the hangin'?'

He packed a full carton of cartridges into a capacious carpet bag, along with some bundles of dollar bills still wrapped in their original paper bands. She grinned.

'Ya aimin' t' buy a stick of candy or somethin' when we get t' Yella Rock?'

'Who knows?' He covered the money with a couple of clean shirts as he continued to explain. 'I don't ever intend t' be short of a buck when I need it. That money could save our lives ... you know that.'

'If that pushy sheriff recognizes us, we'll need more than a hefty bankroll to protect our hides. You'd better pack me an extra six-shooter, along with more bullets. Just in case we have t' make a break for it.'

'Too bad we can't take the Winchesters along,' Frank remarked, doing as his sister suggested. 'But I suppose totin' a couple of carbines would look a mite suspicious to our tame legal eagle.' He began to laugh.

'What's tickled you?'

'Nothin', only thinkin' what JC would say if he knew the real truth. I wonder if he'd be as keen to have us as clients?'

The stage trundled in from the southern trail. It seemed to the Dobsons that everyone from more than a hundred miles away had come to town. Both liveries had 'Full' signs prominently displayed, and everywhere, horses were hitched in cramped bunches to anything their reins could be wrapped around.

The saloons were crammed to overflowing, and stupefied drunken bums sat on the edge of every sidewalk, their hats held out, pleading continually for hand-outs. The whole place was alive with a noisy, carnival atmosphere.

Even the entrances to side streets were blocked off by medicine shows. Fire-eaters, exotic dancing girls and fortune-tellers, all competed for the attention and dollars from the happy-go-lucky crowds.

Temporary deputies were visible everywhere, their eyes peeled for lawbreakers plying their trade. It had always been the case at trial or hanging times, when throngs were most dense, the pickpockets would be dipping for wallets.

· At last the stage made it through the crowds. It pulled up and rocked to a stop outside the depot office. The passengers disembarked. Stiff, dusty and overawed by the abnormal bustle, they collected their belongings and went on their way.

'It's fortunate I telegraphed ahead to book rooms,' JC told his clients, leading the way up wide wooden steps into the hotel, next door to the stage office. 'We'll settle in then maybe pay a visit to the jailhouse, have a chat with the sheriff and take a good look at the prisoners.'

'No, not us. Sylvie's not too good on stage coaches. All that rockin' an' swayin's got her feelin' a mite sickly and tired. And we want to stay in the background. After all, that was the general idea of you dealin' with the reward.'

'As you wish.' The attorney gave a meditative grimace and nodded. 'If that's how you feel.' He smiled and gave a shrug of his shoulders. 'But if you should change your minds....'

'We won't,' Frank answered. 'Feelin' like some shut-eye myself. It's too hot out there and besides, we hate movin' among crowds of noisy drunks.'

The Dobsons remained in the hotel rooms all

night, through the morning, and most of the afternoon.

'Wonder what's takin' that jury so damned long to make their minds up?' Frank asked for the umpteenth time as he paced the carpet. 'Yesterday, JC told us it was all cut and dried. A sure-fire case for the prosecution.'

'Maybe it's that new judge he was talkin' about. Could be he's wantin' t' make a name for himself,' Sylvia suggested as she sat by the open window and cooled herself with a Chinese fan.

In the street below pandemonium broke out.

'Looks like it's over,' Sylvia exclaimed, stopping her fan in mid air and sticking her head out of the window to see further along. 'Yeah, everybody's comin' out of the courthouse. People are fist fightin'. I ain't seen nothin' like it.'

In a moment Frank was at her side, his face white and his hands gripping hard on the sill.

'Hey, you,' he yelled to a youth running below the window. 'What's happened? Is the trial over?'

'I'll say it is,' the excited lad responded. 'Not guilty. The judge said their alibi was too strong and couldn't be ignored.' With that he took to his heels again and quickly disappeared from their sight.

Stunned by the unexpectedness of the news, Frank closed the window to shut out the noise. As if in a trance they stared at each other. Sylvia began to cry silently, letting her tears fall at will. Her brother gritted his teeth as his rage fermented.

'They ain't gettin' away with it,' he growled. 'I want the two of 'em dead, and that's what they're gonna be.'

There was rapid knocking on the room door.

'Come in,' Frank yelled, louder than he had intended.

JC entered. He closed the door then looked across at Sylvia. She hurriedly dabbed at her eyes and cheeks.

'So you know already,' he said. 'I'm sorry, but it's just one of those things which happen sometimes.'

'They got away with it. They ain't gonna hang.'

'No, Frank. They won't hang. Not this time,' the attorney agreed. 'But they certainly didn't get off with it altogether.'

Frank and Sylvia turned interested faces towards him. She was the first to ask the question.

'We heard the verdict was, not guilty. What d'ya mean by ... *Didn't get off with it altogether*, eh?'

Light dawned on JC. He cheered up.

'They were cleared of murder but convicted on other charges of armed robbery. They won't swing but they'll have ten long years to reflect on it in the county prison. In some ways I feel they'd be better off dead, than breakin' rocks in the desert.'

'I want 'em dead,' Frank Dobson stated with venom.

'And that goes for me.' Sylvia moved close alongside her outraged brother. 'We don't want 'em loungin' in no easy-goin' hoosegow. Those bastards have got to die ... d'ya understand?'

Feeling awkward and unsure what he should

say in reply to his unusual clients, JC hooked a finger and ran it around inside his stiff shirt collar.

'Yes, I do understand how you both feel. You're deeply disappointed and I'm sorry about that. But it's the law.... The judge put his interpretation on the case, explained it to the jury and they found the defendants not guilty of murder.'

Absentmindedly, he scratched behind his right ear.

'I must admit, that verdict surprised me too. But look on the bright side. Those criminals didn't escape justice, did they? Ten years' hard labour, are ten years of hell, in anyone's terms.'

'Bull shit!'

'I beg your pardon?' The attorney, unused to such treatment stood aghast.

'Frank means, the law around here stinks.'

'But it's the same law all over the country.'

'Well, mister, it ain't the law for us. Just you tell us what you're due. We'll settle your bill ... now!'

Ten miles out, south-west from Yellow Rock, the Dobsons waited in a derelict and abandoned cabin, built in the shade of Bear's Head rock. This colossal wind-carved edifice stood out on the skyline, a landmark for travellers, visible for miles in every direction. Like a gigantic sentinel, it guarded the restricted opening to Rattlesnake Gulch, and the narrow trail which wound a tortuous path through it to the alkali desert and the county prison.

To the rear of the cabin, a perpetual spring fed a modest-sized water-hole. This was the last chance for more than eighty miles, for anyone crossing the sun-scorched flats, to top up their canteens or water butts.

The two horses, a chestnut and a grey, they had bought at the livery less than an hour after having paid off the astonished attorney. Then they had bought two brand new Winchesters.

The animals stood ready saddled, in a make-shift stable. They had nothing to do, except lick the salt off each other's hide, or flick their ears and swish their tails to disperse the swarms of flies which tormented them.

Inside the shack, Frank and Sylvia waited by the glassless windows which overlooked the trail from the town. An air of deep depression had hung over them ever since they had learned of the ridiculous verdict.

'I feel sick,' Sylvia stated, breaking the long interval of silence which had endured.

'What ya been eatin'?' Frank asked, his eyes never shifting from the trail to town.

'Don't mean that kind of sick. I mean I'm down in the mouth with this whole Max Boylan business.'

'Well, you're the one who was all fired up an' wanted t' do things your way. Ya wouldn't listen t' me.'

For some time she didn't answer.

'Frank.'

'Uhuh?'

'Don't let's blast them no-account killers at the same time.'

For a second or so, he diverted his attention from outside to consider her words.

'I don't get ya. What ya mean?'

'Just what I said. Instead of you an' me both shootin' at different fellas ... let's knock 'em off one at a time. Shootin' together at the same target.'

He mused for a while then permitted a slow smile to spread across his features.

'Good idea. That way we both get to kill 'em, and it'll frighten the shit out of the one who gets shot last.'

'And that's got t' be Boylan,' she insisted. As he nodded, she smiled and perked up. 'Right. We're agreed then?'

'Sure, but don't take it as carved in stone. If we can't do things exactly that way, because of the guards, we'll just have t' manage the best we can.'

'But we'll try it that way first?'

A cloud of dust floating above the trail indicated that the prison wagon and escort were heading their way at a smart lick.

'Another half an hour,' Frank estimated, 'and it'll be party-time again. Bust open them boxes of shells and put 'em handy. I'll check on the horses and fill the canteens, in case we have to stay longer than we intend.'

When he returned with the canteens dripping wet to keep the contents cool, his sister motioned him over to the window.

'It sure ain't gonna be as easy as we thought,' he groaned. 'Ten men ridin' guard, and the wagon driver sittin' alongside that loud-mouthed pig of a sheriff.'

The prison wagon, pulled by a team of four, was little more than a heavy-timbered, open buckboard, with a substantial iron cage built on top. Inside this, Max Boylan and his side-kick Patch, were wrist-shackled to a centre rail, each in full view.

'Do we do things as planned?' she asked as he settled down alongside her and grabbed his newly bought Winchester.

'No, there's too many of 'em. We've got to stop them far enough away, and out in the open, to give us a chance to gun 'em down.'

Sylvia poked the muzzle of her carbine out through the vacant window frame. Methodically she flicked the backsight up and carefully set the range.

'I sure wish we'd had time to sight up these guns properly,' she grumbled. 'I like t' know what I'm usin'.'

Frank ignored her gripe and settled down to be as comfortable as possible under the circumstances.

'When the wagon draws abreast that big old cactus, you be ready on aim. I'll say, "Now!" and you drop the lead horses. Leave me t' take care of the driver and the sheriff.'

The convoy came on without altering its speed. The rifles steadied and settled on targets.

'Now!'

TWELVE

Like a double thunderclap the sound of the rifles crashed and rolled into the distance across the plain. The left-hand lead-horse dropped like a stone, bringing the prison wagon to an abrupt halt. Before the animal next to it knew what had happened, Sylvia's second bullet laid it next to its partner.

If the driver saw the first horse die, he never said anything, but simply tumbled sideways. He was already dead before crashing face-first into the dust.

As Frank's second shot sped on its way, one of the two remaining horses reared up white-eyed with fright, accidentally covering the sheriff and taking the bullet instead of him.

Firing from the saddles of their bucking horses, the guards galloped in all directions, each man doing his level best to remain alive.

The sheriff had deserted the wagon seat and was on one knee using the front corner of the wagon as cover. In desperation he yelled to his men.

'The cabin – they're in the cabin!' As if to prove his words, he shot towards the old shack with his handgun but was hopelessly out of range.

One of the escort, more foolhardy than the others, charged, firing rapidly from the saddle. Sylvia lined up and picked him off with ease. The horse galloped on but its rider slouched in the saddle, dropped his carbine and fell under the pounding hooves. Trampled, he rolled aside and lay still.

She snapped off another shot, and scored another hit, bringing him down as he withdrew a rifle from his saddle holster. But he picked himself up and scuttled for cover, leaving the rifle where it fell, worried only about his left arm which trailed limply at his side.

Three guards on foot, one of them hefting a big-bore Sharps rifle, ran like jack-rabbits, weaving a course to join with the sheriff behind the prison wagon. Only two made it. The third man, the one with the Sharps, did a kind of floppy cartwheel as Frank's lead drilled his chest, and he ended up in a heap like a pile of dirty washing on top of his unfired weapon.

'Ya get the sheriff?' Sylvia asked, her eyes sparkling again.

'Naw, a dang-blasted horse at the back of the team got in the way. But it won't again.' Having said that, he swung the carbine up and shot the last luckless draught horse through the white blaze on its forehead. It dropped dead, leaving a clear field of fire at the prisoners exposed and cowering inside the cage. 'There, now we might see what we're firin' at.'

'When I get me back to town,' snarled the sheriff, 'I'm goin' to see the mayor. I'll tell him in real plain words, exactly where he can shove this damned five-pointed star ... and I hope it hurts.'

'Oh, in that case, if you're doin' that,' the deputy put in hopefully, 'will ya put in a good word for me, Sheriff?'

The senior lawman gazed pityingly over the bags of wrinkled skin beneath his bloodshot eyes, at the lanky narrow-shouldered deputy, and sniggered in his face.

'Me, put in a good word for you? Hell, boy, I wouldn't recommend you as kindlin' for the devil.'

'Hey, Sheriff,' Max Boylan called out from inside the cage above. 'Ya can't let us stay in here and be shot t'death by some bushwhackers.'

'Huh, who says I can't?'

'This ain't justice, ya rotten bastard,' the convict screamed.

'If there was any damned justice,' growled the lawman, 'I'd be back in town, organizin' the gallows and gettin' ready t' hang the both of ya, t'morrow.'

A bullet struck an iron bar close to the corner of the prison cage. It deflected and removed half the deputy's right ear. He yelped like a slapped girl and on seeing the bright red blood splashed all over his shirt, almost fainted.

'I've been hit, Sheriff ... I'm bleedin' t'death.'

'So ya are,' the sheriff confirmed with hardly more than a glance in his direction. 'Now be quick. Stop foolin' around. Get this blasted wagon unhitched and freed from them dead horses, before I shoot ya myself ... properly.'

'But ...' whimpered the shaken deputy.

'No buts,' the sheriff warned. 'Do it.'

'What they doin' by the wagon?' Sylvia asked as she reloaded the Winchester, her nimble fingers pushing the cartridges into the magazine as easy as another woman would knit. 'Why they movin' that?'

'They've hardly any cover out there and they need to get closer so they can use their handguns on us.' He settled down on aim again. 'Can ya see that Patch guy? He's the one on the left inside the cage.'

'Yeah, I can see ... we takin' him now?'

'After a count of three. Stand by.'

She lined her sights on the one-eyed captive and waited for the count.

'One ... two ... three!'

With great satisfaction they watched Patch half stand and slam hard against the iron bars. Then he dropped, leaving his hands up in the air, suspended on the middle rail by his manacles.

'One to go,' murmured Sylvia. 'But let's wait. Don't shoot Boylan yet. Let him sweat a while.'

Unseen by the Dobsons, one of the guards had worked his way around the flanks to a spot close to the base of Bear Rock. Once there he climbed to a ledge which overlooked the window where Frank and Sylvia fired from.

'I'll have to stop 'em bringing that wagon up to act as cover,' Frank said, settling down to draw a bead on those pushing it.

A sudden loud thwack. The carbine seemed to leap from Frank's hands and fell outside the window as he cried out with pain. His face and shirt front were bathed in blood.

'Frank!' Sylvia was at his side in a moment.

'It's all right, Sylvie. I'm OK. A bullet's smashed the butt of my Winchester and filled my face with splinters.' He began to pluck the offending slivers of wood from his flesh. 'If ya can get the ones out of my cheek, I'd be obliged and able t' use a rifle again.'

More bullets entered the cabin, shattering more of the empty window frame and tearing into the floor. Forced to keep their heads down by this new turn of events, she set to and quickly pulled out the worst of the splinters.

'I think I got me one, Sheriff,' the sniper from the ledge shouted. 'I can see his gun dropped outside the window, there.'

'Good man. You keep 'em busy for a minute, will ya, Jake?'

'You bet,' Jake answered confidently and another magazine of cartridges was emptied into the window space.

'Keep down and hand me yer carbine,' Frank demanded. 'I can see the backshootin' bastard up there, on that second ledge.'

'Ya get anybody that time?' the sheriff yelled. He sounded closer.

'Wouldn't be a bit surprised,' Jake called back. 'There ain't anyone shootin' at ya, is there?' He was laughing as he poked his head up over the spur of rock on the ledge.

Frank's forefinger, sticky with his own blood, closed on the trigger. The butt kicked back against his shoulder. Jake stopped laughing and flopped over the end of the ledge. On the way down his face caught the first ledge and was unrecognizable, even before he smashed on to the rocks beneath.

A fusillade of shots peppered around the window and the wall behind the Dobsons as those outside vented their fury over Jake's death.

Frank had moved away from the window and gazed out through a split in one of the boards. At once he saw that the guards had managed to bring up the wagon as a shield. They had more cover the closer they got to the cabin. Their daring increased with their confidence, as the handguns came into range.

Each time bullets were fired from inside the cabin, many more were returned. The shots were coming in from different angles, pinning the Dobsons down most of the time, and adding to the danger.

'Let's get out of here,' Frank called to her as she fired out from a gap near to the door. 'I'm down to my last few shells.'

'Me too. But we can't go yet.' She looked

surprised that he should say such a thing. 'We haven't got Boylan.'

Unable to get a clear shot at the county's newest convict, Frank moved to the back wall and slowly stood until he could see out across the room and through the window space. Boylan was crouching inside the cage, making himself as small as possible.

'This is for Ma an' Pa, Frank,' Sylvia reminded him. 'So do it good.'

The shot from the Winchester struck Max Boylan's belt buckle and drove it deep inside his guts. His scream drew the attention of the guards who turned to gaze without pity, as he writhed in agony inside the cage for a long ten seconds.

Sylvia took the carbine.

'This time, kill 'im,' her brother told her coldly. 'We gotta go.'

Her shot finished the screams and their quest for revenge had ended.

'Come on, let's go.'

Someone fired blind from outside. Frank's legs gave way beneath him, and he sat heavily on the dirty floor.

She was down on her knees, her arm around him to give support, almost as soon as he had reached the ground.

'You been hit?'

'I … I don't rightly know. I can't move, but I can't feel nothin'.'

'Can ya stand?'

He tried hard. She could see that, but even with

her pulling he could do nothing to help himself.

'Hey, you in the cabin.' They both recognized the sheriff's voice. 'We've got you surrounded on all sides. Come out peaceful-like, I'll see ya get a fair trial for what ya did.' He waited for a reply but when none came he continued. 'I'll give ya two minutes to throw out yer guns and come out reachin' high. If ya don't, we're comin' in with guns blazin' to take ya dead or alive.'

Sylvia felt her hands warm and wet. They were covered in her brother's blood, from a wound in his back.

'I don't want t' hang, Sylvie,' he whispered hoarsely as she held him close. 'Will ya help me? If I can just get to my horse....'

Hot tears stung her eyes as she sat and rocked him like a baby, with his bloodied face cradled next to her own.

'Sure I'll help ya, Frank.' Her voice was soft. She sniffed and gave him a brave smile as she kissed his brow. 'Yer my big brother ... there ain't anyone gonna hang ya ... or me.'

Frank did not make a sound. He just slumped in her arms soon as the derringer fired. She stroked his hair sadly and, placing the bleeding gun to her own head, she whispered one last word.

'Goodbye.'